I0740150

PANHANDLE MAYHEM

PANHANDLE MAYHEM

TROUBLES IN LOVE-LAND BOOK TWO

J. M. ANTON

J. M. ANTON

Half Appy Press

Copyright © [2015] [J.M. Anton]

The moral right of the author has been asserted.

All rights reserved.
No part of this publication may be reproduced, stored in a retrieval system, or transmitted, in any form or by any means, without the prior permission in writing of the publisher, nor be otherwise circulated in any form of binding or cover other than that in which it is published and without a similar condition including this condition being imposed on the subsequent purchaser.

This book is a work of fiction. People,events,locations, and situations in the Troubles in Love-Land Series are purely fictional and any resemblance to actual persons, living or dead, is coincidental.

Published by Half Appy Press

ISBN: 978-0-9962645-1-8

Typesetting services by BOOKOW.COM

FOREWORD

Alexandra Parker and Melinda Potter travel far from home to meet Melinda' online Romeo. Alexandra takes an instant dislike to David Decker. He was attractive with his cornflower blue eyes, dark hair, and engaging smile, but there was something sinister about him.

Have you ever wondered why some people avoid online match services? Melinda Potter's experience will answer that question within the pages of "Fateful Waters" the first book in the Troubles in Love-Land Series.

Alexandra reluctantly agrees to travel to Texas with Melinda. Alexandra turns up missing after a flash flood nearly claims her life. The two friends suffer a multitude of mishaps when they end up thousands of miles from their Ohio homes.

Lexie battles several advisories and her attraction to a tall dark cowboy as she tries to extricate Melinda and herself from the clutches of the drought-stricken panhandle. She summons Melinda's father for help.

Book one ends with Lexie cutting short her bookkeeping job at the Rocking R when she and Cutter Ross' cook/housekeeper nearly come to blows. Cutter is used to rounding up strays and when we leave him he is out to recapture his stray bookkeeper.

Acknowledgments

Editing by the contributing editors at "Another Set Of Eyes."

A very special thanks, to Kellie Anton for editing of the German language inclusions.

Cover design is by Goddess Fish.

Thank you to the readers of Book One who have requested a copy of this sequel.

CONTENTS

CHAPTER 1

SEPTEMBER brought a few cooler days accompanied by spits of rain to remind Lexie that fall and winter were around the corner. It also brought Cutter Ross to Ohio. His rental vehicle came to rest in the drive alongside a modest home with light gray vinyl siding accented with maroon shutters, trim, and asphalt shingles. He took note of all the green shrubs, and the abundance of colorful mums that surrounded the house as he made his way up the walk and front steps. He sucked in a fortifying deep breath before knocking on the door. A gray-haired, grandmotherly, version of Lexie answered his knock and he introduced himself.

"Hello, Mr. Ross! Lexie will be home shortly; she's out with Skip. Please come in. I'm Jane O'Rourke, Lexie's grandmother."

He wondered if she was a black belt too, given that she wasn't the least bit concerned about inviting a stranger in to her home. She served him coffee and warm apple pie. As if Lex's grandmother was able to read his thoughts, she set his mind at rest about strangers merely walking in. "I don't usually let people I don't know sit at my kitchen table, but Lexie has told us so much about you, and described you in such detail that I feel like we already know you."

"Did she tell you what a jerk I am?"

"No. She must have left that part out. She only told us she'd straightened out your books and then came home."

*****

A short time later, the biggest German Shepherd he'd ever seen bounded up the steps from the small landing that led to the back entrance off the kitchen, effectively ending the conversation with Lexie's grandmother. The huge dog skidded to a halt, braced his legs, and with his hair standing on end, curled up his lip to show off his razor-sharp pearly whites.

"At ease, Skip. *Sitz hin!* He is a friend, I think."

Skip sat at Cutter's lost bookkeeper's command, but kept a wary eye on the stranger at the table.

God, she was a sight for sore eyes. He suddenly realized that he had not met the real Alexandra Parker. She eyed him with almost as much distrust as her dog was displaying before asking, "Are you lost, cowboy?"

"Yes ma'am, I was hoping you could route me in the right direction."

She looked him over skeptically. "Come off it, Cutter. What are you really doing here?"

Skip was on his feet and growling. He picked up on the hostility in his mistress's voice. Once again, she calmed her threatening dog, speaking what sounded suspiciously like a German dialect while she fixed a glass of tea. Then she sat down with her grandma and her unexpected guest. She was about to shovel through his crap and get to the bottom of Cutter's motivation to grace them with his presence. Her thought process was derailed when Skip hightailed it to the front door. "I guess that means Mom is home."

The dog was hopping up and down like a huge wind-up toy. He didn't stop until the auburn-haired, green-eyed beauty greeted him. She spoke to the dog in the same language her daughter had just used to command him. The new arrival patted Skip's huge head before she joined the rest of the family in the small kitchen. Much to Cutter's amazement, Lexie's mother was at the most twenty years older than her daughter.

Cutter was beginning to appreciate the big dog in this household of pint-size women.

Lexie was about to make introductions when her exuberant mother did the honors herself. "Well, I'll be damned! Cutter Ross, Right? I'm Eve Parker." She reached out a perfectly manicured hand to clasp his warmly, much as her mother had done earlier. It was easy to see where Lexie inherited her sense of style as well as her colorful language. "I wondered who the Yukon in the drive belonged to."

Lexie had entered through the back gate at the rear of the fenced in backyard and missed the strange vehicle toward the front of the house. She gave him an *are you crazy* look he'd come to know quite well.

"You didn't drive here did you?"

"No, it's a rental."

Cutter invited the trio to dine with him at a restaurant of their choice. No big surprise, Lexie chose a popular seafood place. It hadn't escaped his notice that she often would avoid the beef dishes and the steaks Maria had prepared for dinner. Instead, she had opted for the sides of salad, rice, and vegetables. Eve poked in the number to the restaurant for call ahead seating while Lexie and Grandma Jane changed clothes, and then Lexie's mom settled in to interrogate him.

******

Lexie would have loved to know how and when Cutter had convinced her mother that she should spend her Saturday playing tour guide for him while he checked out some farms near the Williams place. She'd protested, in vain, that the Williams boys would be better guides. Cutter argued that the whole project had been her idea and the least she could do was follow up. His argument had been unanimously upheld. She wouldn't know a moment's peace for a week from Mom or Grandma if she'd been rude enough to refuse to accompany him. Skip wasn't happy that he couldn't come along, but he was better off at home. She didn't want poor Skip to get into trouble for taking a chunk out of him, if Cutter really aggravated her. She was still out of sorts about his reaction when she'd inquired whether or not he had the funds to tackle the hay field lease project.

It was obvious to Cutter that she was still holding a grudge, for what she considered his assumption she'd been after his money. She hadn't said a word since they left the house. He decided to make a wrong turn at the next intersection.

"Cutter! You needed to go left, not right."

"Are you sure?"

"Yeah. I'm sure. I've been out this way hundreds of times." She wondered why he didn't use the GPS, but then she realized what little use it had been to her out in his part of the world. She figured he didn't trust the device.

"Right, Bill Jr. told me that when you were in high school you used to be one of the kids that helped his dad put up hay when he baled."

"Some of us have to work for other folks. At that time in my life, I preferred to be outdoors, and Mr. Williams boarded my horse at a reasonable price in exchange. He got most of my pay back anyhow."

"Is that the horse you sold when you went to college?"

" Yes. I got a partial scholarship, but school was expensive. He has a nice home with three little girls who spoil him."

An hour later, she was ready to strangle him! He pulled in the drive only to be met by both Bill Williams Sr. and Jr. who quickly piled into the back of the Yukon. She absolutely did not need to be there. Following a lengthy tour of Williams' most productive of his threatened leases, Cutter and the Williams duo made arrangements to meet on Monday to look at a couple of options to secure the chosen hay fields. Not once was she consulted or asked for an opinion.

Alone once again in the rented vehicle, Cutter made a circuitous sweep of the nearby area. They broke for lunch close to one that afternoon. Lexie routed him to her favorite lunch spot for soup, bread sticks, and salad. The prices weren't as attractive on the weekends, but she reasoned it would not bankrupt him. Still, the not-so-frugal decision weighed on her conscience. Cutter handed her an envelope with the Rocking R logo emblazoned on it while they sipped on their choice of beverages and waited for their lunch order. With all the caution due the unearthing of a rattler's nest, she opened the sealed flap. Enclosed was a check made out to her for the amount of eight hundred dollars. "What is this for?"

"Reimbursement for your ruined clothing."

"Isn't this excessive? I distinctly remember stating the value of the outfit Maria trashed as slightly over three hundred."

The subject of the settlement was resumed after the salad and bread sticks arrived, and the waiter was out of earshot. "The balance of the repayment is complements of a fat, happy, little calf that wouldn't have survived if you hadn't jumped in the muck after him. You also lost a pair of shoes in that rescue, if my memory serves me correctly. I haven't the slightest idea what women's apparel sells for, so I estimated based on the value of the green outfit."

"Honestly, Cutter, the loss of that outfit and navy pumps was my own fault. I probably wouldn't have lost them in the mud if my temper hadn't gotten the better of me."

"Whatever—the memory is priceless. Take the check, Lex. It is my last official task as your employer."

He watched her fold the check, placing it in the old leather wallet, and then she returned it to the back pocket of her snug fitting jeans. That was when she threw him a curve ball.

"Have you found a new bookkeeper?"

"Sam has taken over the interviews while I'm away. It is an ongoing search."

"I hope you won't take this the wrong way, but I wouldn't hire another woman while Maria is in charge of the house. Also, if the new bookkeeper finds discrepancies in Mr. Henson's record keeping, give him the benefit of the doubt before you take offense."

He let her bombshell regarding his family's longtime bookkeeper slide for the moment. He had more pressing matters to resolve before returning home. Instead of following up on the accounting of years past, he brought her up to speed on the current negotiations with owners of the leased hay fields. He ended his narration as they took to the road again by asking her opinion.

"Cutter, my opinion doesn't matter, if it ever did. I'm no longer in your employ, so it's not my place to approve or disapprove of how you handle the ranch business. I do think your horses and cattle will appreciate your efforts and be able to weather the interminable drought much better. But isn't this overkill, even for you? What are you going to do with all the stored hay? It could combust and take out other buildings along with the hay barn."

"I don't plan to store it any length of time. The Rocking R isn't the only outfit in the area trying to outlast the drought. I intend to resell it to others at a reasonable price. What I would like to do this afternoon is talk to a few small farmers that are in danger of going under. It occurred to me that while here I could find a supply of corn and oats in addition to the hay. Our local crops have withered in the fields and aren't good for much but fuel for spreading wildfires. Even if the drought ends soon it's going to take a while for things to get back to normal."

They spent the afternoon talking to farmers located near the hay fields under negotiations. Cutter made deals to lease three farms and buy two, letting the families that were involved stay in their homes as caretakers. He agreed to pay them to farm the land for him. On the way back home Lexie's economical nature got the better of her.

"Cutter, this is really getting complicated. Do you have a good corporate attorney on retainer who will be able to guide you through this project? This has gone way beyond leasing of the hay fields that I'd envisioned."

"The Rocking R still retains the same attorneys my dad had used for ranch business. Their advice was not to tackle it, but they're old school, in a lot of ways, and still think I'm just a dumb cowpuncher who doesn't know how to do anything else. I haven't connected with anyone here, yet." He withheld the information about his personal lawyer, and the corporate law firm in Dallas that he had on retainers.

"You need to make a connection before Monday. You know, Williams will have a lawyer in tow on his end. Do you trust me, Cutter?"

"With my life, darlin'."

"Okay, two things. One, quit with the endearment crap; this is business. We're discussing your money, not putting your life in my hands. Two, do you trust me with your money?" "With every penny, Lex."

It was odd, but the shortening of her familiar nickname had annoyed her at first. However, lately she found she missed the sound of it. Not another soul on this earth called her Lex. She banished the retrospective thoughts from her mind when Linda Potter answered the call she had just placed. "I hate to disturb you on a weekend, Mrs. Potter, but it is kind of urgent that I speak with your husband."

Cutter continued to drive while listening to one side of the conversation. She had the ear-buds on, which made him privileged to only her questions or responses. He recalled meeting her friend Melinda at the hospital in Amarillo; Potter was her last name.

"No. I didn't make it today. Mr. Ross showed up unexpectedly. I will run up after church in the morning. Right, he's that Mr. Ross. It seems he is bent on leasing or buying half the farms in this part of Ohio, and I thought that Mr. Potter may have a bright young attorney on staff who would be able to handle complex business negotiations including real estate deals. Thanks, I'll pass along the invitation." She disconnected, and then turned to Cutter.

"You have another dinner invitation. Also, Mr. Potter is visiting Mel and will probably return my call later this evening. I will give him your cell number so that you can discuss options and, if you are comfortable with his firm, you can hire them to guide you through the Ohio laws governing the kind of transactions you have in mind."

Cutter had barely shifted the Yukon into park in the drive when Grandma Jane opened the front door, letting Skip escape. "About time you two got back! I thought you may have eloped or something."

"Gram, for God's sake! This was a business trip." Lexie turned her attention to her exuberant dog. "Okay, Skip, go get your leash."

Jane hooked the leash to the excited dog's collar when he bounded back onto the front stoop, but she couldn't resist getting in another dig. "Yeah, right. Monkey business. Dinner will be ready in an hour. Don't dawdle."

Lexie bit her lip and settled for rolling her eyes in exasperation as she and her two companions walked toward the small park at the end of the street. Cutter appeared to take her grandmother's comments with more grace. He chuckled at her presumption. Less than a block away from home and her buttinski grandmother musical tones announced an incoming call.

"Thanks for returning my call so quickly. How is Mel today? That's excellent! I was really worried about her. Around ten or ten-thirty, it depends on how windy the priest is in the morning. Sure. He's right here."

Lexie handed the phone and ear-buds to Cutter, and then took off to play with her dog to give him a bit of privacy. It sounded like Mel was on the mend from Lexie's brief conversation with her friend's father. The loss of the baby that she hadn't even known about until she'd miscarried had sent her into another bout of depression. That unfortunate turn of events really stoked Benson's quest for vengeance.

Cutter caught up with her and Skip. They spent nearly an hour wandering around the park before returning for the evening meal.

Dinner went off without a hitch or any more kibitzing from either of her outspoken elders. Arrangements were made to meet at the house at nine thirty the next morning. She was to make introductions at the hospital and visit with Mel while her father and Cutter went off to conduct business.

Lexie settled in to work after he left for the evening. She was way behind with her online assignment. She'd been frustrated at the time, but with the recent demands on her time she was relieved that her temp assignment had ended the prior week. The funds the job had provided helped to pay for her online classes, but it had curtailed the ability to really study the material. She was beginning to doubt she would ever pass her CPA exam at the rate she was going. It was nearly four the following morning when she could no longer keep her eyes open. Her head had barely dented her pillow when Gram's voice called up the stairs to jolt her back to consciousness.

"Lexie, your handsome cowboy is pulling into the drive."

"Give him some coffee and a couple of muffins, Gram. I'll be down in a few minutes" she answered.

How could she have overslept? She was sure she had set her alarm. Okay. I need to concentrate on basics — shower cap, a quick shower, brush teeth, a little make up, blue pullover. She was making a mental inventory. "Damn!" Lexie pulled her arms back out of the sweater to apply the forgotten deodorant. With her arms back in the sleeves she brushed her hair, tied it back with black scrunchie, slipped into her black pumps, picked up her black shoulder bag, and went downstairs for a much-needed cup of strong coffee to jumpstart her day. Halfway between her room and the stairs, a draft on her legs caught her attention. "Oh, my God! I am really sorry I missed Mass this morning. Please don't let this be an omen of how this day is going to unfold," she prayed as she hurried back to her room to kick off her pumps. She slipped on the black slacks she'd forgotten and stepped back into her shoes. Lexie took the time to check out her reflection in the full-length mirror mounted on the inside of her closet door. Satisfied that she hadn't forgotten anything else, she made the second attempt at descending to the main floor. The mere thought of how she almost made her entry caused an unwelcome heat to rise from her feet to the top of her head. Lexie likened herself to an old fashioned thermometer with the mercury rising. Visions of everyone's reaction to her near wardrobe malfunction as well as the humiliation of showing up to greet Cutter, in that state, had her face glowing with a monster blush. She descended the stairs more slowly than her grandmother usually did. Lexie hoped the slow pace would give her a chance to regain her composure.

CHAPTER 2

Composure regained, and her professional woman guise back in place, slightly less than two hours after the near-miss with a slack-less breakfast appearance, Lexie introduced Cutter Ross to Mel's dad.

"Mel, I think you already met Cutter."

"Yes, hello again, Mr. Ross. It seems to me that the last time we met was in another hospital."

"I remember our first meeting very well."

"Whatever happened to Mrs. Ross?"

"Unfortunately, she was the product of a paperwork snafu."

Lexie hadn't expected Mel to bring up the Mrs. Ross debacle in front of her father. Once the men had adjourned to Potter's law offices Mel started with the inevitable forty rapid-fire questions.

"What is he doing here, Lexie?"

"I think he's trying to stake a claim to a large portion of Ohio farmland." Her answer was a little flippant, but she didn't feel comfortable talking about Cutter's business dealings with anyone.

"Is that the only thing he's here to stake a claim on?"

"I can't imagine why else he would travel here from Texas."

"Yeah, well, you should see the way he looks at you when he thinks you aren't aware. I would sell my soul and give up my inheritance to have a man look at me that way."

"Oh, I think you've had the look you so vividly described. I remember at the time thinking, 'turn around Mel, there's Mr. Right', but you were otherwise occupied and oblivious."

"Who?"

"The day you get released from here. I will tell you. How you deal with the situation is up to you, but you need to be stronger and get back to your old self."

"Well…don't let your Mr. Right get away by hiding under your independent, self-sufficient woman-of-the-business-world mask, Lexie. He didn't think twice about giving you his name when it counted. There must have been some connection there before that. He really doesn't strike me as the type to give any random good-looking woman his name to get her admitted to a hospital."

Before she could respond, Mrs. Potter entered the room. Lexie sighed as if relieved of a crushing load when Mel dropped the subject. But what she had said kept playing in Lexie's mind. She still didn't remember what had happened after Cutter deposited her near the Escalade that fateful June evening; she vaguely remembered losing her phone in the mud, and two cowboys rescuing the newborn calf, but then nothing until she awoke in the hospital. She figured she might never fully remember the interim.

Mel's familiar complaints about hospital fare struck a chord, and interrupted Lexie's side trip down memory lane. "Mrs. Potter, is Mel's diet restricted?"

"No. She's allowed to eat pretty much anything. Why?"

"I brought her something I know she likes, but I wanted to ask first."

Lexie withdrew a small container from her shoulder bag, handing it to Mel. She took the lid off smiling and rolling her eyes. She quickly stashed the container of blueberry muffins under her bed sheet when her Mom questioned the contents.

Mel, declared, In her best imitation of a little girl, "MINE!" Her mother laughed so hard that tears spilled over.

"Well, gee, Mom. You don't have to cry about it. I guess I could let you have one."

Lexie made the trip down to the lobby to give Mel and her mother some time alone. She thumbed through the unseen pages of a nameless magazine while she waited for the universe to issue its next twist in her life. Mel was right; there had been some connection there the very first time she had seen him appear out of a downpour like a wraith. The mere sound of his voice had elicited chills. At the time, she'd shrugged it off as her soaked condition and fogging mind. That initial meeting aside, she found herself drawn to him. Then he had rescued her again, after Mel had evicted her, and the attraction had grown.

Lexie lost track of time searching the archives of her memory banks for clues. She and Cutter really weren't the least bit compatible. Grandma always told her that opposites attract, but they don't last. Mom held the opposite view and claimed it sure had been great while it lasted. Mom reacted as if Grandma's point of view was a personal dig at her, and Lexie's long dead father. She wondered if her grandmother's viewpoint was because her grandparents had been at odds most of the time, like she and the boss of the Rocking R. As if she had conjured him up, Cutter arrived with Mr. Benson Potter.

She ended up sharing reheated beef barley soup and roast beef sandwiches with him at their small kitchen table. Once they'd left the hospital, he offered to buy her another meal out, but when she refused, he gave her that "I hate to eat alone" line. They had the place to themselves, with the exception of one happy dog parked at her feet wearing a hopeful expression as she sliced the roast for their sandwiches. Skip knew his mistress was good for a couple of handouts of the mouthwatering meat that beat the heck out of the dry food in his bowl. Once she was seated at the table, Skip laid down, but kept an eye peeled for food that periodically fell from the table; Lexie was particularly prone to dropping food more often than his other housemates.

Cutter frowned, and Lexie took it as a sign of disapproval. "Haven't you ever had a dog?"

"When I was a kid, but he wasn't allowed in the house."

"Why not?"

"Maria's mom was our cook and housekeeper, back then, and she pitched a fit about filthy animals in her kitchen and dirtying up the house. She claimed to have enough to do, cleaning up after Dad and his two unruly sons."

"Were you unruly, Cutter?"

He only grinned, raising one dark brow for emphasis. She made the comment that at least they had that much in common. While Cutter devoured a slice of apple pie, Lexie cleaned up and loaded the dishwasher. Skip trotted down to the landing to return with his leash dangling from his mouth.

Cutter empathized with the hopeful fleabag hopping up and down, his tail wagging like mad, all for a little attention from the center of his world.

"I think Skip wants to go out for a walk. Would you mind taking him out back while I slip into a pair of jeans?"

He wasn't at all sure that the dog would go with him, but the poor guy must have been home alone for quite a while, and was in desperate need of relief; Skip rocketed through the door as soon as it was opened. The dog dropped his leash just outside the door and continued to make record time to a small square of gravel at the rear of the cyclone-fenced yard, where he took care of business. That necessity out of the way Lexie's canine wonder returned to pick up his leash.

"How are you guys getting along?"

"I think he was ready to bust a gut. He must have been confined in the house alone all day."

"I was up until the wee hours of the morning working on my online prep course for my CPA exam, and overslept. I usually take him out in the morning, but you were already here, and I was not functioning very well yet. I forgot to remind Gram to let him out."

They strolled to the end of the street, turned left, and kept walking. Skip stopped occasionally to christen a worthy tree or fire hydrant. Cutter was amazed by how green the grass was, and the abundance of colorful shrubs and flowers this late in the year. It was sure a different universe than the one he lived in.

"What kind of dog did you have, Cutter?"

He was lost in comparing the pros and cons of the worlds where they had grown to adulthood. It took him a moment to recall what was fast becoming ancient history. "He was a mutt. I guess he'd been some kind of a hound mix. Less than half the size of this guy."

"Mutts and half-breeds are some of the best dogs. What did you call him?"

"Red Baron."

"I'll bet he looked like Snoopy, right?" He nodded his head in reply, but looked as if he expected a rebuke. "That's great! It shows a lot of imagination. Most kids would have tagged the puppy Snoopy. Did you have him a long time?"

"No. Less than two years, I think. I was only about seven or eight at the time."

"Did he get hurt? I lost my first dog when a car hit her."

"No. My dad shot him."

"God, Cutter, that really sucks! Why did he kill your dog? Did he contract rabies?

"Something got into the hen house and killed a couple of chickens; the rest of them wouldn't lay for a week. Juanita told Dad that Red Baron had done it."

"Was he bloody, or have other signs of a kill on him?"

"I didn't see him. He was already dead and buried when I got home from school. The only blood I saw was on the back step where he'd been killed."

Lexie didn't know what to say. What a horrible experience for a child! No wonder he had frowned when she told him she had a dog. Now, she was grateful that she didn't wait for her belongings, including Skip. Maria, like her mother, would probably have pitched a fit over a dog in the house.

Back at home, Skip was checking out the tires on the rental while they made plans to meet late Tuesday for dinner with the Potters. She was totally unprepared for him to wrap her in his arms and kiss her senseless. It was becoming difficult to take a breath, and her heart was bruising the inside of her ribs. In self-defense, she pushed away from him. Still breathless, all she could manage was his name. "Cutter?"

He pulled her closer again and whispered in her ear. "I've wanted to do that since I first saw you."

He went for an instant replay, adding tongue for a little added attraction. She was completely out of control, and latched onto his invading tongue as her body melted into his. Cutter was the one who managed to hold his passion in check, and he broke the carnal embrace. Lexie was mortified by her abandon of proprieties smack in the middle of the lighted driveway, for the entertainment of the neighbors. She picked up Skip's leash, mumbled a good night, and made a quick retreat through the front door. His soft chuckle echoed in her ears even after she closed the door and he was a long way down the road. Parts of her body she was unaware of until tonight were still humming and throbbing. Lexie had occasionally dated since high school, enjoying some intimate moments, but she was always in control. Nothing in her experience compared to the earth-shattering encounter of being kissed by Cutter Ross.

"I don't know, Skip, but if Cutter wasn't a man of his word, I might not have made it home. How the heck am I supposed to get out of that dinner with the Potters on Tuesday night?"

She tried to regain some self-control. By rote, she went through the routine of a house check: Mom and Gram were in their rooms, next lock the doors, fill Skip's water bowl, and turn off the lights. Lexie was all ready to burrow under the covers when the musical notes of her phone blasted like a full symphony orchestra in the silent house. She snatched it up, quickly silencing it. Oh, God! It was Cutter! She let it roll over, and was about ready to put it back on the charger when it vibrated in her hand. This time she poked it, and answered in a hushed voice, "What?"

"I wanted to make sure everyone was safely home."

"They are all sleeping. At least I hope they are all still asleep."

"Sweet dreams, Lex."

"Go to sleep, Cutter."

******

While Cutter and Mr. Potter were negotiating high finances the following day, she was visiting with Melinda. Lexie was the bearer of a much larger container of baked goods this time. She also purchased two large glasses of tea, complete with accordion-necked straws at the cafeteria on her way in. A peek inside at the contents of the huge vessel sent her friend into peals of laughter.

"Wow! Are you trying to put me into a diabetic coma?" Mel inventoried the confections: oatmeal cookies, brownies, chocolate chip cookies, and macaroons. "When did you bake all of this, Lexie?"

"Last night. I couldn't sleep, thanks to a certain Texan's twisted sense of humor. All my online work was caught up, and I was too agitated to read, so that left baking. Anyhow, you don't have to eat it all at once."

Mel was intrigued; it was unusual for any man to have much of an effect on Lexie's focus. "What did he do?"

"Just as I was ready to snuggle under the quilt Gram made at her quilting bee, the one she gave me for my birthday when

I turned twenty-one, he calls, and ends with 'sweet dreams'. I mean he…knew damn well I wouldn't be able to sleep after that."

Mel was munching on a nut-filled brownie while contemplating exactly what she was hearing. "That doesn't sound so bad. Why would that keep you up all night?"

Lexie stared at her friend, selected an oatmeal cookie, rationalizing it as the breakfast she'd skipped, and then washed it down with a long drink of tea. She set her drink back on the adjustable bed table they were sharing and gave her friend a very graphic description of the scene in the drive the night before.

"I told you he was here for more than one reason. But no, you didn't want to acknowledge the hot looks cast your way. Well, Lexie, you can't hide from the truth any longer. You've found Mr. Right."

"Cut the Mr. Right crap, Mel. It wasn't anything other than pure animal magnetism. The man is loaded with it."

"So, you admit you're attracted to him."

"I don't deny that. Still, it's no excuse for losing control. Thank God I don't have to see him, or try to avoid the prospect today. I don't think I can face him."

"Aren't the two of you going to dinner with Mom and Dad tomorrow night?"

"Don't remind me. Actually, I was thinking of taking a trip up to Kelly's Island, and keeping a large part of Lake Erie between us until he goes home."

"Come on, Lexie, you're not a coward. Are you going to let him get away? You'll regret it the rest of your life if you do."

"Mel, I know you're a hopeless romantic, but let's get real here. Cutter and I are diametrically opposed. I mean talk about opposites attracting! We would be at war constantly."

"Are you sure? The two of you looked pretty comfortable together the few times I have seen you in his company."

"All that aside, Mel, there is no way in hell that I am ever going back to Texas. I hate the place."

"You can't hate the whole state, Lexie. You only saw a small part of it during the worst drought in a century."

"Do you watch the news at all? It's not only the drought and wildfires; drug traffickers run their poison unchecked across the border and onto private farms and ranches. They threaten the owners and their families."

"Lexie, you know we have more than our share of crime in Ohio. Instead of drought, we have flooding of rivers and creeks, but we have a lot of the same problems."

"Stop trying to rationalize things, Mel. We don't have rattlesnakes, or Maria Rodriguez."

"I know. It is kind of a role reversal. You're usually the rational one trying to keep me from over-reacting. Who, the hell, is Maria Rodriguez?"

Lexie caught her best friend up on the events leading to her quitting her bookkeeping position at the Rocking R. She stayed until mid-afternoon, when Mel's Mom showed up. On the trip home, Lexie decided to splurge and spend part of the recompense from the Rocking R on a new dress for the following night. She blew the whole wad and then some, and she still had a hair appointment that was not in her short-term plans or budget.

Back home again, she showered, climbed into her long-neglected bed, and blanked out, not surfacing again until Gram sent Skip to retrieve her for dinner. Halfway through the meal, Gram burst her hard-won tranquility.

"Alexandra, do you think that it is appropriate to carry on with your cowboy in our drive? If you can't control your baser instincts, at least seek some privacy. I am sure you are the talk of the whole neighborhood today."

"God, Grandma, it's not like we were humping in the damn drive!" Lexie was really hoping that no one, especially her grandmother, had caught last night's performance.

"Don't use that tone and nasty language with me, young lady! You will have to atone to the Lord for using his name in such a context."

Her mom glared at Gram. Then Mom inquired what she had done with herself for the day, after her pre-dawn baking spree.

"I spent most of the morning as well as the early afternoon with Mel. Then I went shopping and blew a lot of money I don't have to spare on a new dress for tomorrow night. It had to be altered in the bust and shortened, so I have to pick it up in the morning."

"Oh, I wish you would have called me. I could have taken a long lunch and gone with you."

"Sorry, Mom, it was a last minute decision. Mel kind of talked me into it. I really was thinking of canceling the whole thing; you know how I hate dinner at the Potters' country club."

"It wouldn't be very hospitable to leave Cutter in the lurch when you've already accepted as a couple, and if he went alone, I'll bet he wouldn't stay that way long."

"Yeah well, if someone wants him, they can have him. Actually, I'm still thinking of taking a vacation trip alone, and coming back after he returns home."

"You don't want to do that, Lexie. You will regret it the rest of your life."

"Now you are starting to sound like Mel."

Evelyn Parker took a sick day, so she could escort her daughter to the dress shop for the final fitting. Lexie brought along a pair of gray leather pumps that she had purchased the day before. She had to admit the dress was worth every penny. The soft, shimmering, gunmetal gray creation hugged her like a second skin. A high turtleneck collar was contrasted with a diamond-shaped cutout placed just beneath it and ending enticingly slightly above her bust. Sleeveless, with a low-scooped back, the dress flowed from her hips to the tops of her new shoes. The skirt was split on the right side from her knee down, allowing free movement.

"Lexie, you will be the belle of the ball."

"Yeah, well, you know what happened to Cinderella at midnight."

Lexie asked her mother drop her off for the hair appointment. Eve continued to shop while the beautician worked on her daughter. She had seen a dress that was the answer to her search for something special at the shop where Lexie had picked up her beautiful dress.

******

Cutter called Lexie about six to say he was running late. He had to negotiate terms for the dinner. It seemed that Mr. Potter wanted to pick them up in a limo, and Cutter wanted his own vehicle, so the two of them could come and go on their own time schedule. Lexie could only imagine the confrontation when the two powerful personalities squared off. Benson Potter was the hands-down champion at that kind of persuasion, but it appeared that Cutter won the face-off. She replaced her gold studs with a pair of single pearls. It was a trick putting on the long dress, even with her Mom's help, without messing up the intricate French braid that cost as much as some of her college texts had. She consoled her thrifty nature by reminding herself that the cost and tip were helping to stimulate the economy. That excuse was beginning to wear as thin as her shrinking bank account; she'd also used the same rationalization when she bought the dress and the shoes. By the time she slipped into the soft leather pumps, Mom returned with her beautiful, gray fox jacket.

"This will go perfectly with that dress and protect you from the cool night air."

"Thank you." What else could she say? She was having trouble not tearing up and ruining her makeup, so she settled for giving her mom a big hug. Lexie prayed that she wouldn't turn into a small urchin in rags with Mom's gorgeous coat transformed into little gray foxes running for the hills. Fortunately, she didn't have much time left to conjure up more negative scenarios.

Cutter looked as much a fairytale character as she did, dressed in a navy western suit with darker yokes. The white shirt and navy tie contrasted, big-time, with his perpetual southwestern tan. They arrived pretty much on time, and as he handed over the keys of the rental to the valet she wondered if he would have been so blasé about surrendering them if they had been for his own vehicle. The fantasy couple was escorted to the Potters' table after she reluctantly checked her mother's jacket. The Potters were already seated, including Mel who was flanked on the right by her father and on the left by Booker. Cutter destroyed the boy-girl rotation by seating himself between Lexie and Booker. He wasn't particularly discreet in his suggestion to the maître d'—"the lady prefers the other chair"—when the headwaiter attempted to pull out the chair to seat her next to Booker. Cutter's stated seating change sounded more like a growl. Booker merely grinned, but Mel broke out in delighted laughter.

As she took her reassigned seat next to Mrs. Potter's right, she confronted her friend. "Why didn't you tell me earlier that you would be here, too?"

"Mom and I had a bet going whether or not you would show up, and I didn't trust her to tell me the truth. I also offered to fill in for you, just in case, so they sprung me for the night, and if I don't do anything outrageous, I might get out for good."

"Well, laughing like a loon at your best friend is not a good start, Mel."

"Lexie, you look so beautiful and sophisticated. Doesn't she, Booker?"

"Absolutely ravishing. A veritable feast for the eyes! Don't you think so, Cutter?"

Cutter frowned at the culprit who had admitted to him earlier that he had transported Lexie from the ranch to the airport. "I wouldn't have taken you for flowery speeches."

"One must learn to adapt and blend in with their surroundings."

Lexie didn't miss Booker's wink in her direction with his last comment, and neither did Cutter. His jaw had developed that ominous tic, and his previously warm gray eyes took on an icy hue. Pent up tension melted away when their waiter returned for the newcomers' drink order, and to offer the menus. Lexie ordered a White Russian made with Coke. Cutter ordered scotch, neat.

"Have one for me too, Lexie. I'm not allowed—medications, release rules and all that, blah, blah, blah. That was our favorite drink whenever we went out to one off the country-western dance clubs while we were at OSU. Down in Columbus, they call it a Colorado Bulldog. If you order it that way in here, they either don't know what it is, or they get their fancy drawers in a twist." Mel directed the last bit of information to Cutter.

"I plan to have several more. If these two decide to go at it, I plan on being too drunk to care about the outcome or the humiliation."

Cutter ignored Lexie's jab at his small altercation with Potter's bodyguard, and concentrated on the pretentious French plastered all over the ornate menu. She must have misinterpreted his scowl, and assumed that he could not decipher it. She leaned over and lowered her voice.

"Order in English, and if you want beef, the prime rib is much better than the steaks."

He wanted to haul off and kiss her enticing, pink-stained lips, but figured she would object to a public display of affection.

After dinner and another round of drinks, the mellow dining music changed and the dance floor began to fill up. Lexie was observing some of the interesting gyrations of the teenage group. Music and dance, like fashion, changed in a blink of an eye, and if you didn't keep up you got left behind. Then the music changed to slower, more intimate selections, and the floor shed most of the previous dancers to be replaced with couples like the Potters. She was pleasantly surprised when Cutter asked her to dance. Halfway through the second piece of music she inadvertently insulted him.

"Cutter, you are a good dancer. Who knew?"

He held her away from him at arm's length, so he could look into her blue eyes. "You really have a low opinion of me don't you, Lex?"

She maintained eye contact. "That's not true, Cutter, I wouldn't be here right now if that were the case."

He must have been satisfied with her response; he urged her much closer, and his calloused hand moved lower on her back. Lexie decided she needed to cut off her drinking binge; three, and she was overheating big-time. Thankfully, the music changed again and the teens reclaimed the floor. Cutter escorted her back to the table, but she picked up the clutch purse that matched her shoes, excused herself, and then headed for the ladies' powder room with Mel following in her wake.

After recycling her water intake, Lexie washed her hands and freshened her makeup. She glanced at her friend's reflection in the wall-sized mirror above the washbasins.

"How are you holding up, Mel?"

"Really good. The food sure beats the hell out of the hospital slop. So far, it has been very entertaining."

"I noticed you only danced once, and I know you love to dance. Is it too much for you?"

"Have you ever danced with your father?"

"No. I never knew my father, or at least not that I can remember."

"Sorry, I forgot. But dancing with my dad is not a real hoot."

"So let's shake things up a little bit. Ask Cutter to dance with you, and I will dance with Booker."

"Shake things up? You mean start a war. Cutter will go after him."

"No he won't, because you'll explain to him that Booker and I are merely old friends."

"Cutter isn't going to want to dance with me."

"Sure he is. He is a man, and you are a beautiful woman. If he should be reluctant, promise you'll tell him something about me that he doesn't know. But first go flirt with the band; find out if they have some line dance tunes in their repertoire."

Lexie returned to her seat, but Mel kept going around the edge of the dance floor. Mr. Potter was about to go after her when his wife restrained him. He directed his attention and his question to Lexie.

"Where's Melinda going?"

"To request some special tunes."

He sat back down but kept a watchful eye on his daughter. Booker hadn't taken his eyes off of Mel since they re-emerged from the ladies room. Cutter reluctantly agreed to dance with Mel, but he was less than happy about Lexie's plan to dance with Booker. As planned, on the next set of slower music she latched on to Booker and dragged him on to the dance floor, right behind Mel and Cutter. A couple of songs later, they were all back at the table while the dancers changed again. Absently, Lexie picked up her drink and downed some. She noted that Cutter had switched back to coffee.

The music stopped, and the bandleader announced a twenty-minute break. During the break, desserts were ordered

Twenty minutes flew by while she tried to explain the planned trip, in response to his question about why she would want to go out to the middle of the lake. She hoped to God that Mel hadn't told him it was to wait out his inevitable return home. That was the first thing she asked as she and Mel took to the dance floor, dragging Booker with them. Cutter declined to join them when the band announced a set requested by Melinda Potter.

"No. I didn't tell him you were thinking of turning tail; I only mentioned you were planning a trip out into the lake for a few days."

Cutter was enjoying the view. The two ex-roommates were having a good time; it was obvious that they had danced together quite a bit at the local establishments that catered to the college crowd. They hadn't stopped talking since they took the dance floor. Booker on Melinda's right would occasionally roll his eyes, or shake his head at parts of their conversation. It amazed him that the guy could be taking in their chatter, continually scan the room, and yet never miss a step.

Cutter managed one more dance before Lexie called it an evening. She used the excuse that she was worried Mel wouldn't leave until they did. He went to reclaim her jacket while she thanked his new lawyer and his lovely wife. He held the jacket while she slid her arms in. "Thank you, Cutter."

If he were Skip, he would be wagging his tail and wanting to do the trick again just to see the warmth in her eyes, to have her smile at him once more, and thank him in that soft quiet way. She gave Melinda a hug, then turned to Booker, took hold of his hand, and leaned down to whisper in his ear.

"Always, Lexie."

*****

Cutter curiosity got the better of him. "What did you say to Booker, Lex?"

Standing under the portico in front of the Country Club, waiting for the valet to retrieve the SUV, she responded through chattering teeth. "I asked him to look after Mel.

God it feels like it wants to snow. It's a good thing Mom convinced me to take her fox jacket."

The valet showed up and one of the others on duty opened the passenger side for Lexie. She slipped in and cranked up the heater while Cutter took care of the dual tip. At the first stoplight, he shrugged out of his jacket, and by the second he'd removed his tie and opened his collar. Lexie started to laugh, like someone was tickling her. Cutter figured she'd had one to many drinks. "What's so funny Lex?"

"What time is it?"

"A couple of minutes past midnight."

"Aha, the witching hour when all the princesses and princes turn back into their true form."

She stroked the fox jacket, and then unhooked her seat belt so she could remove it and place it in her lap. Cutter noticed that she continued to pet it. "Lex, are you warm enough now that it's alright to turn down the heat?"

"Oh, sure."

"Put your seatbelt back on."

"I will as soon as I let them go."

"Let who go?"

"The little foxes inside this jacket. They should appear any minute."

He pulled over at the next opportunity, and took the jacket away from her. He was worried she could decide pitch it out the window. He put her jacket on the seat behind them with his before refastening her seat belt.

"Christ, Lex, you're hammered."

"Boy, don't say that in front of my grandmother. Unless you're up to a lengthy lecture on the inappropriate use of the Lord's name."

He pulled the vehicle into the drive and manually doused the headlights. He slid across the seat and reached to undo her restraint, after releasing his own safety belt. She smacked his hand. "What do you think you're doing, Cutter?"

"Trying to unhook your seat belt."

Once she was released, he drew her into his arms and kissed her with all the passion that had been building since his first taste of her Sunday night on this very spot. Again, it was he who broke things off. He wasn't sure she was coherent enough to be consensual, and he didn't want their first time together to be in this rental. "Lex, I'm not much for flowery speeches, but I want you to come home with me."

"You mean to the hotel?"

"That would be great for starters, but I was thinking of something more permanent."

"You want me to go back to Texas?"

"Yes. I'm asking you to marry me, Lex."

She didn't say anything in what seemed like forever. "Cutter, that's really nice, but this isn't me. It's all only make believe."

"Damn it, Lex. I fell in love with you the first time I put my hands on you and pulled you out of the muck, soaking wet and covered from your head to your bare toes with it."

That declaration took her by surprise, and her thought process was a bit impaired. "How soon were you planning to begin our wedded bliss?"

"As soon as we can get a license and work through the rest of the rigmarole."

"Cutter, I need to sleep on this and tackle it with a clear head."

"Sleep on this." He kissed her until she went limp in his arms, and then slipped a ring on the third finger of her left hand. He got out of the Yukon and opened the back door to collect her gray clutch and her mother's little gray foxes, still in jacket form. He walked her to the door, opened it with the keys from her purse, handed them to her, and guided her inside with orders to lock it behind him. He closed it and left.

She absently patted her dog's head and locked the door. "Come on, Skip, let's call it a night. I drank way too much, and I probably pissed off Prince Charming."

CHAPTER 3

Eve Parker's voice echoed painfully between Lexie's ears, "Good morning, Cinderella!"

An equally evil being glued her ridiculously heavy eyelids shut. Blind, hampered by lead arms and legs, she made a valiant effort to navigate the familiar route to the small bath that she knew was attached to her room. OOPS! Hopping on a throbbing big toe, she felt her way along the slowly material-izing wall until she found the opening. Washbasin located, she splashed cold water over her face; the remnants of the sticky substance hampering her vision that the pain in her toe had managed to crack melted away with the water bath. Only semi-blind with water dripping down her face she managed to find the towel rack. The image staring back at her from the looking glass seemed to be in as bad a shape as she was. Mirror girl must have had a long restless night too, and not found any sleep until well past dawn. She stared with mounting dread and a queasy stomach at the hand of the reflection still holding the small towel to her face. A diamond reflected the overhead light and sparkled back at Lexie. Slowly she gazed at her own hand, and there it was!

"Shit! It really had happened. Now what the hell are you going to do?"

She was cussing at her reflection when her mother returned, all bright-eyed and cheerful. An unsolicited audible groan escaped from somewhere deep within when she caught the cheerful face of her mother behind her own horrified reflection.

"That must have been some shindig, Lexie. I do believe you are hung over."

"Could you tone down the cheer? It's giving me a headache. If you want to be helpful, see how good you are at removing the high-priced knots in my hair. Maybe washing it in the shower will send the rest of this nightmare down the drain."

Eve didn't say anymore as she undid the lovely braided work. Lexie's reaction was not what she'd expected from her newly engaged daughter.

Nearly an hour later, closer to lunch than breakfast, Lexie made what felt like a grand entrance into the kitchen to a duet of good mornings. It was so weird. She wouldn't be totally surprised if they were to break into song. The whole scene was otherworldly and totally out of character for her elders. She got a glass of water to down a couple of ibuprofen, found handful of oatmeal cookies on a tray—thawed reminders of her baking binge— and popped one in her mouth. Then she put the rest on a small dish, made herself a cup of tea from the still-warm ceramic teapot, and carted her sparse breakfast back to the table. Their eyes had been on her ever since she entered the room. She sat at the table and attempted to ignore the goofy grins and concentrate on feeding her jumpy stomach. Finally, she gave up, and after a fortifying gulp of warm tea, she confronted them.

"Okay, why are the two of you still sitting at the kitchen table at this time of day with goofy smirks on your faces?

"Mom and I are waiting for the news."

A little more tea was called for, and one more cookie. Lexie wished the ibuprofen would kick in already. "What news?"

Her response snapped what patience Gram had left. "Alexandra, we want to know about last night."

"Dinner was good. We all danced, and I drank too much. Now I'm paying for my overindulgence."

"Lexie, what your grandmother meant is that we want to hear about Cutter's proposal and your obvious acceptance."

"What makes you think I accepted?"

"The diamond on your finger, for starters."

She gazed down at her hand as if an annoying bug had landed on it. She shrugged, feigning indifference. "I didn't really accept it, he kind of shoved it on my hand. I might have dented his male ego when I told him I had to sleep on it, and tackle his proposal with a clear head."

"What was there to think about, Lexie? The man obviously loves you, and from the stories you've told us about him and your time in Texas we assumed you felt the same way."

"Yeah. There wasn't any point in rehashing the crap, was there? Anyway, it's moot. We'll probably never see him again."

"I doubt that. He's called twice this morning to check on you. He said you weren't answering your phone."

"I left it on silent mode, and it's probably still in my purse."

"Cutter also said he got tied up with some real estate deal and wouldn't be here until afternoon."

"Great. I was kind of hoping he got mad enough at me, this time, to go home." She snatched her jean jacket off one of the pegs on the landing along with Skip's leash, and stormed out the back door.

Jane shook her head at her granddaughter's strange behavior. "She sure is on a tear, Eve. Not what you would expect."

Lexie ran nearly double her usual two miles before backing off to an easy jog. It was making her crazy. She loved the man, but really didn't want to spend the rest or her life on a ranch in the middle of nowhere, fighting heat, dust, drought, and Maria Rodriguez. She looked down at her dog. Mom and Gram took care of him while she was at school, but they didn't run with him. They didn't take him to the park, to the lake, or on car trips. If she left him home, he would be confined to the small fenced backyard. He could easily clear the four-foot fencing, but he wouldn't unless he sensed danger to one of them. Wherever she ended up Skip would be there too.

By the time she returned, the rental was parked in the drive, and Cutter was parked at the kitchen table. Grandma jumped down her throat as soon as she opened the door, and before she had even hung up her jacket or Skip's leash. "It's about time you returned, Alexandra. Get cleaned up—lunch is almost ready."

She greeted Cutter, excused herself, and went upstairs to take a quick shower and change her sweat-soaked clothing. She prayed he wouldn't bring up anything personal over lunch. They needed privacy to have this discussion. Mom must have gone to work, leaving only the three of them for lunch.

Upon her return to the kitchen, she refilled Cutter's coffee and talked with him as she made herself tea and cut fresh French bread to go with the chicken vegetable soup simmering on the back burner. "How did the land purchases go?"

"Most of it went off without a hitch; it's down to a matter of banking and escrow. But the bigger grain farm we looked at never went through probate or transfer of title when the original owner's passed. Now, there's a frantic search being conducted for their parent's last will. In addition there's an ongoing dispute about a boundary line with a neighbor."

"Sounds like you had a lousy start to your day."

He shrugged his shoulders before he buttered the bread, placing it on the small plate she'd provided. Lexie carried the bowls to the table after Gram ladled the soup into them. When they sat to join him, he resumed the conversation. "Either Benson will get it sorted out, or I'll have to scout out another grain farm. Booker suggested Benson check into the status of the disputed neighbor as a substitute, or an add-on. How are you doing, Lex?"

"I've had better days. I had a monster of a hangover this morning, but I'm much better. Serves me right partying and drinking for two."

Lexie's reference of doing something for two brought Jane's wandering thoughts back to the present, but she got it completely out of context. "Alexandra Parker! Don't tell me you are pregnant!"

Cutter almost choked on his soup. Lexie got up to pat him on the back, and wondered how she could perform a Heimlich on him given their size discrepancy. She gave her grandmother a disapproving look very similar to the daggers that the matriarch was now throwing at Cutter. He seemed okay, so she didn't have to try any heroics.

She knew that her grandmother's mind wandered from time to time, but Lexie was aggravated at her grandmother's assumption. "Okay, Gram, the answer is no."

"No, what?"

"No. I'm not going to dignify your insult with an answer."

Jane O'Rourke threw her napkin on the table, rose, and stomped out of the kitchen, muttering something about "how she never."

"Yeah, you did, Gram! Neither Mom nor I would be here if you hadn't."

"Clean the kitchen, you little strumpet, before you go off on your next tryst."

Lexie made quick work of the cleanup, and then she, Cutter, and Skip escaped in the rental, bound for a park. When they arrived at the Rocky River Reservation of the Metro Parks, she latched on to her dog's leash attaching it to his collar. Lexie answered Cutter's questioning expression.

"Technically, dogs are supposed to be on a leash in the park. Once in a while I risk a citation and turn him loose, but he loves to play in the river. I have a mat for him in the back of my Suburban, but he would make an unholy mess of the interior of the Yukon. The rental company would most likely charge you so much as a cleaning fee that you could buy it. Anyway, I thought this was a more private setting for us to talk."

"Does that mean you've thought it over and come to a decision? You're still wearing the ring I gave you last night, and haven't thrown it at me. So I am taking that as a good sign."

"It merely means that I am giving it due consideration. Do you want Mr. Potter to draw up a pre-nup?"

"Lexie, whatever is mine will be yours."

"You mean you no longer consider me a gold digger?"

"Are you going to hold that against me for the rest of my life? No, I don't think you're after my money. In some ways, I think I would have a better shot with you if I didn't have a dime."

"The thing is, Cutter, it's not something you instinctively felt. This change came about after you researched me backward and forward, like I was applying for a high-security position. Right?"

"Lex, I fell hard from the beginning, but I thought my feelings for you could obscure my common sense. After you flew back here, I talked to a few of your friends."

She found a park bench away from the few Wednesday afternoon senior citizens enjoying what remained of the trees and wildflowers. She decided honesty would serve them best. "First, Cutter, I love you too."

His heart almost leaped out of his chest. He waited her out, sensing an objection coming.

"But I'm not sure that is enough to overcome the hatred I have for Texas."

"Lex, you can't hate the whole state!"

She laughed at his response. "That is almost word for word Mel's reaction when I told her the same thing. But I've lived in your home, and I am not sure that I want to spend my life in that hostile environment."

Cutter had a feeling she was going to object to his longtime friend, "You want me to fire Maria?"

He sounded appalled at the idea. This was her way out! Instead, Lexie found herself reassuring him that she hadn't meant Maria in particular. "I know that your cook/housekeeper is more like family than just another employee." He appeared to relax at her concession. Maria was a huge compromise on her part. The absence of the cook in Lexie's prospective new home would have been the deal clincher. She was still uneasy about making a commitment that would drastically change her life. "Okay, Cutter you keep

Maria, and I keep Skip with me, in the house."

"If we are negotiating terms, let's compare apples to apples; you can't compare Maria to Skip!"

"When you're right, you're right. Skip is much better mannered, loyal, and definitely not a backstabber, but I am willing to concede the point. They definitely are not equal. Do we have an agreement on this item, Cutter?"

"And if I don't agree to your terms? How many are there by the way?"

"If you don't agree to the other three, since I caved on the biggest obstacle to my return to the Rocking R, you can go home to Maria, and I will stay here."

"Let's hear the rest of your list."

"First, I want my old job back with same pay scale agreement."

"You don't need to work."

"Yes, I do. Besides, the books need to be kept, and I'm good at it. So, why hire someone else? You draw a salary; why shouldn't I? I have to do something or I will go nuts."

"Agreed. What's next?"

"I want to buy another horse."

"There are plenty of horses on the ranch, Lex. Take your pick."

"No. I want my own horse not one that belongs to the Rocking R, and like Skip, it goes where I go. So, when you decide you made a big mistake and throw me out, they go with me." She waited for him to agree before she moved onto the last item. His jaw was clenched, the tic was back, and he growled for her to continue. Maybe I should have left out the part about throwing me out, she thought. His whole amused attitude along with his sense of humor faded into the annals of history.

"Cutter, I deferred to you on the cook/housekeeper issue, but not on this one. You have to agree to at least a one-week vacation each year somewhere green with flowers and lakes, or maybe near the ocean. If you don't want to join me, then I need you to let me go alone. Do we have a deal?"

"Are you sure you trust me to honor the deal, if I agree to it?"

"You would have your ring back by now if I didn't think your word could be trusted."

"I agree to your list of demands. Let's go. I have a lot to do yet, and daylight's wasting."

Daylight is wasting? She wondered if that was an expression he used often. He didn't say another word until he dropped her at the house. "I'll pick you up at nine in the morning. Skip will have to stay at home on this trip."

Lexie guessed that she had ticked him off again, but she needed to have some say in her future; after all, she was the one giving up everything familiar.

Nine o'clock the next morning, he was in the drive, waiting with the engine running. Lexie popped into the passenger side of the warm Yukon. The first serious frost nipped at her nose and ears on the short sprint from the front stoop. He didn't say a word. Not even the usual good morning. Maybe things were not progressing well on the grain farm deal, but she decided not to ask. If he wanted to tell her, he would. "Where are we going?"

"Downtown."

Great! He was back to single word answers. "Where downtown, Cutter?"

"To the county courthouse."

"You can't drive this downtown on a weekday! We'll never find a place to park."

He knew deep down that she would come up with another objection. "Do you know a better way to get down there?"

She routed him to the closest Rapid Station parking area, and they rode the commuter transit rail to the terminal tower. Thankfully, it was much warmer close to the lake, and the walk to the courthouse was pleasant exercise. She was grateful that she was in much better condition than when they first met, and had resumed running, or she wouldn't have been able to keep up with his long, ground-eating, stride.

Cutter was a man on a mission, and it never occurred to him that she was having difficulty matching the pace he'd set, until she stopped dead in her tracks. He halted his forward progress to inquire about the delay. She was winded, and standing with her hands on her hips.

"Where in the hell is the fire?"

He slowed his stride to match hers, as he had done when she began pacing the halls of the hospital in Amarillo. It wasn't an imposition then; he had arrived to spend time with her after putting in a full day of physically demanding work on the ranch. Now, the snail's pace had him about ready to jump out of his hide.

Once he had the required marriage license in hand, he began to relax enough to enjoy the day and her company. They had a lot to accomplish during the three-day waiting period. Blood tests, physicals, and locate a tux that would fit him on short notice. It was Thursday, and by Monday he planned on being a married man.

******

Lexie was discussing her strange day and the sprint across Cleveland's public square with her mom over dinner. Grandma was out with her friends for dinner and a night of fast-paced bingo.

"It was like he was afraid they were going to lock and bolt the doors before we got there. I don't think he took a relaxed breath until we'd signed our names and paid the fee. He isn't used to sitting for hours driving, only to sit some more negotiating deals. Cutter is used to working on the ranch pre-dawn until nightfall. I think it's wearing on him. His sense of humor is fading, not to mention, he is growling more and more."

"His lack of humor and grumpiness wouldn't have anything to do with you, would it?"

"Some—well, maybe a lot. He wasn't overly happy about my negotiations before I agreed to marry him."

"Did he agree to your requests?"

"Three and a half out of four."

"For God's sake, Lexie. How do you get a half?"

She explained about the Maria versus Skip compromise while she refilled their teacups, and cut a slice of still-warm apple pie for each of them.

Eve processed the information about the cook at Cutter's ranch. She wondered why her daughter hadn't mentioned the woman's hostility before. Lexie's reluctance to accept Cutter's proposal made more sense to her now. Eve reasoned that her daughter must really love him to even consider going back there. Maria would probably be more civil when Lexie returned as Cutter's wife. Still, she had a feeling that more was going on than her daughter was sharing with her. She knew Lexie had said all she was going to about her reluctance to return to Texas. "Where's Cutter having dinner tonight?"

"I think from what he told me he has a business dinner with Mr. Potter tonight. Then he mumbled something about Benson or Booker routing him to a place that would be able to fit him for a tux on short notice, which means I need to find a wedding dress!"

"Why don't you do the dishes and clean up while I check with the dress shop where you found the gray dress? I saw a couple of wedding gowns in there that you might like. If they are gone, I'll call around to see what is available elsewhere. I'll take a half day tomorrow, and we'll shop for a gown and have lunch." Eve was looking forward to the shopping trip and spending some time with Lexie. Maybe she could coax her tight-lipped daughter to share what else was bothering her.

Lexie knew that she'd been played when the shop owner greeted her mother by name. Mom had been in on this from the beginning. She wondered whom else Cutter had enlisted to his cause. It was her fault they all thought that the Rocking R was one big happy family. She didn't see any point in dwelling on the negative. Mel was the only one besides Cutter who had some idea of the animosity she was subjected to that finally sent her packing until she'd spilled the beans to Mom. Booker was the only one who knew about Decker's sick fixation on her, unless he shared the threats with Mel's dad. Lexie said a private prayer that she was strong enough to cope with it and the daily life on the ranch. I'll probably have ulcers before I am twenty-five, she speculated.

*****

Sunday, a little over a week since he had shown up on their doorstep, Cutter had dinner with them. Plans were for a limo to pick up Lexie, her Mom, and Grandma to transport them to the Potters' church for the impromptu wedding ceremony. Then, the limo would take them all to the country club for a quickly organized reception. But Cutter was annoyingly silent about the post-reception plans, and if either of her elders were privileged enough to know, they were mute. He joined her and Skip for their habitual after-dinner walk.

Mel had agreed to be her bridesmaid. Lexie had very recently found out about the rest of the Potters' involvement, and she was a bit uncomfortable about it. "How did the Potters get so involved with this, Cutter?"

"Your Mom and I were having trouble locating a church on such short notice. The plan was to have a quiet ceremony and a meal afterward. I happened to mention the problem to Benson, and told him that I guessed we would have to settle for a Justice of the Peace. He said he would check with his pastor, and they came up with the Monday afternoon slot. Your Mom was thrilled with the church idea, so I accepted his offer."

"You know that is a Lutheran church don't you?"

"Not really. Does it matter, Lex?"

"Not if it's okay with you. But it has made me realize how little I really know about you."

"Are you having second thoughts?"

"God, yes! Second, third, fourth, and on and on. Nerves aside, how did we go from a small dinner to the Potters' country club?"

"Mel and her mother got together with your Mom, and now we have a reception."

"It's still going to be a small gathering, right?"

"At this point, Lex, your guess is as good as mine."

When she groaned out loud, Skip stopped inspecting a large oak near the entrance to the small park, where their wanderings had taken them, to determine the cause of her distress. Cutter scooped her into his arms, and they were tangled up again. Skip sat at her feet with his head cocked to one side, trying to figure out this new development.

The arrival of a large family group allowed Lexie to come up for air and try to regain her wits. They walked home hand in hand, and his kiss goodnight left her knees weak. How was she supposed to get any sleep after that? She was going to look like one of the walking dead stumbling down the church aisle tomorrow. Lexie laughed at the mental picture. Everyone was worried she would pull a runaway bride routine, but one look at her zombie-like appearance would more likely send the groom heading for the hills. Was she still searching for a reprieve? It was too late now. She was about to marry the stranger who had claimed her as his wife in the Amarillo hospital, but for real this time.

CHAPTER 4

The hairdresser was late! Gram's and Mom's coiffures were completed and looked fantastic, but she was just getting started. Lexie decided to have a manicure while she waited to have her hair done. Her intent had been to take care of that chore the previous night, but she was such a mess after their mind blowing farewell she couldn't steady her trembling hands.

The prenuptial makeover was a squeaker. They barely had enough time to get dressed before the allotted departure time. Lexie was finishing with a light coat of slightly pink lip stain when her mom came in to announce that the limo had arrived. She stepped into her gown to avoid messing up her makeup or the twists and braids in her upswept hair. Her mother fastened the line of satin buttons that ran from her waist to her high collar. The satin material fit as well as the gray dress had. Her bridal gown also had a high collar, but there the similarities ended. The white satin creation had long sleeves and flared slightly from her waist to fall in soft folds to her satin pumps. She refused to wear a veil. Instead, she had a string of light blue glass beads woven into the back of her elegant hairstyle; that and the hidden garter covered the something blue requirement to placate her grandmother. Single diamond studs sparkled from her earlobes. The diamond earrings had been her graduation gift from her Mom and Grandmother prior to her fateful trip to Texas.

Her hard-won composure slipped when her mom picked up her luggage and garment bag. "I'll carry these down, Lexie. Grab your overnight case. We need to go."

She wouldn't be coming back here… not tonight. Other than to pick up Skip and the rest of her belongings, she would likely never be able to return to the home where she had grown up. The limo was a long, white job that drew a lot of attention from some crane-necked neighbors.

Forty minutes later, it pulled into the side drive of the church. Mel and her father met them and escorted them to the front of the church. An usher Lexie had never seen before winked at her, and then informed everyone that they were about ready to begin. Mom opened a large floral box that had been occupying a long table in the vestibule where stacks of hymnbooks shared the space. From it she pulled a bridal bouquet of orchids and white roses; the box produced a smaller version of the floral creation for Mel to carry.

Mr. Potter escorted Grandma Jane to her seat next to his wife in the front row on the bride's side of the church. They had no more than gained their seats when the groom and Booker, his best man, entered from a large oak door to the right of where she stood looking down the center aisle of a very modern church. The vestibule where she and the rest of the female half of the bridal party waited was the only part of this structure that even resembled the almost century old church that she frequented on most Sundays. The ceiling soared a good twenty feet or more, and was all wood planks and beams. Tall glass windows dominated the wall space, letting in the light and providing a view of the wooded setting that encompassed the exterior of the house of worship.

Lexie peered down the aisle toward the two tall men taking up their positions to await the bride and her small entourage. Her heart was about to jump from her chest and she was having difficulty breathing. She made a superhuman effort to fight off lightheadedness. Tunes of the wedding march replaced the hum of human voices and signaled Mel to lead off the procession. Evelyn Parker waited until Melinda was a third of the way down the aisle before she escorted her daughter to the tall Texan who would whisk her away from them.

Lexie was amazed by how many people were in the church. She didn't know how this Lutheran outfit did things, but she figured most of the crowd was there for a regularly scheduled service following their wedding. As she moved closer to Cutter, she noticed that Booker was watching their progress as intently as Cutter, but if she wasn't in church, she would swear that his focus was on her mom. Mel stepped forward to relieve her friend of the bridal bouquet for the duration of the vows. It seemed, to Lexie, they had been up there in front of the church forever, but on the other hand it flashed by in the blink of an eye. She and Cutter exchanged rings, and then she heard the pastor pronounce them husband and wife. Cutter kissed her right in front of the whole assembly of onlookers. She wasn't sure if he held back, or she was just too terrified and numb to feel the usual impact of his kiss.

As they turned to face those assembled, the pastor said it was his pleasure to introduce for the first time Mr. and Mrs. Cutter Ross. "That's what he thinks!" popped into her head and whispered past her lips. She glanced to her right at Mel, who must have been thinking along the same lines. They both snickered as she handed back the lovely bouquet. The two old friends were failing miserably at controlling their mirth. Lexie felt Cutter squeeze her left hand; she looked up at him to question the gesture. I'm going to have a perpetual kink in my neck, she thought; she barely reached his shoulders and would constantly be peering up into his changeable gray eyes. He leaned down and whispered. "Behave yourself, Mrs. Ross, or I will exact my revenge later."

After the photo session, set up by her mother and Mrs. Potter, they finally made it to the country club reception. The rumbling coming from the center of her being was downright embarrassing; her stomach thought she was attempting to starve it and was making its displeasure audible.

Cutter raised one of his dark brows in surprise—she would love to know how he did that, as she couldn't raise only one eyebrow no matter how she tried—and he questioned when she had last eaten.

"Not since yesterday. I had a few swallows of tea and snagged a cookie on the way out the door this morning. I sure hope they have plenty of food."

The catering was magnificent and plentiful, but the meal didn't appear for nearly an hour after their arrival. However, the champagne flowed like water, and Lexie had a couple of pre-dinner flutes to wash down the cracker and cheese hors d'oeuvres. She passed on the iffy pâté—it looked too much like canned dog food—and she had never liked caviar, so it limited her appetizer selections. She was able to ingest enough to quiet the complaining of her stomach.

It appeared the groom's side of the church had been populated with the farmers and landowners Cutter had brought under the sphere of the Rocking R. He introduced her to everyone, and it amazed her that he could remember the names of each child within a half dozen families. The only familiar faces, to her, within the agricultural group belonged to the Williams family. She was getting a headache trying to remember who was who. Maybe it was more hunger and the free flowing champagne that was the cause? Whatever. At the first opportunity she extricated herself and went in search of her mother.

"Mom, do you have any ibuprofen, or something else for my head? It's killing me!"

She was surprised to see Booker conversing with her Mom, and she would swear there was some chemistry afoot. Mel confirmed Lexie's observation when she found her friend in the ladies' lounge. After freshening up, Lexie kicked off her shoes and collapsed on an overstuffed armchair. "God, Mel, I'm exhausted and famished. I don't know which is throbbing more, my head or my feet. Why are you hiding out in here, Mel? Not that it's a bad idea."

"I thought I would give your mom and Booker a modicum of privacy."

"You think there is something going on there?"

"Could be, they kind of hit it off when he was driving our mothers all over creation this past week while they shopped and planned the wedding. Do you have a problem with Booker and your mom, if something develops between them?"

"Heck, no. I think Booker is great, but Grandma is sure to object. You should have seen the daggers she was throwing at Cutter."

"I thought she liked Cutter?"

"She did until the morning after the dinner party here. I was bemoaning my hangover, and told Cutter it was the last time I partied and drank for two. Gram picked up on the 'for two' and asked me if I was pregnant."

They were having a good laugh at her expense when Jane O'Rourke walked in and suggested they end the powder room gabfest to return to their seats. It appeared that the meal was finally being served.

Food! She managed two bites of her salad before Mr. Potter stood up to make a toast. Well, he actually made several toasts. He started off with everyone toasting the bride and groom. He went on to raise his glass to his wife, Lexie's mom, the pastor, the caterer, and the band for reworking their schedule. Another flute of bubbly collided with her still restless stomach. The servers topped off all the glasses. She quickly buttered her hard roll; the first bite was like heaven in the shape of a round sesame seed bun, but the next bite went down like lead when Mr. Williams stood up to toast his new business partner and the best little hay bucker he ever had work for him. Another quick forkful of salad and Booker made a toast. Thankfully, he was brief, but before she could return to her salad, it was removed by one of the servers. She snagged her partially eaten roll from her small bread plate, as it too was spirited away.

There must have been some kind of a rule she wasn't familiar with that stated a bride and groom were not supposed to eat at their own wedding. Every single time she would put something in her mouth, some sadist would start clanking silverware on a glass, and the noise grew in volume as more people around the room joined in. It didn't subside until the obligatory kiss. After a half dozen instances, Lexie identified the Williams boys as the ringleaders. She stood up threw down her napkin, urged Cutter out of his seat by the lapel of his tux and instigated a hot steamy kiss that elicited a lot of hoots and clapping. She turned to face Bill Jr. and his brother Bob.

"Okay, that's it. The next person that interrupts my meal by putting a piece of silverware to a glass or cup had better be ready to duck one of these crystal rose vases aimed at their head."

Lexie regained her composure and her seat at her grinning husband's side to the cheers of the women in the assemblage. She imagined that a lot of them had probably been through the same torment. She ate only half of her now cold meal, washing it down with the bottomless glass of champagne.

The rest of the evening went by in a bit of a fog. She danced with her new husband, and a few dozen other people. She threw her bouquet to the single ladies, including her mother and Mel. Eve Parker caught the bridal bouquet, and Jane O'Rourke could be heard lamenting, "Oh Lord, here we go again!" Cutter scorched her leg with his large hands while he peeled off the lacy blue garter before tossing it to the single guys. Bill Williams Jr. snagged that little trophy. He slipped it up his left arm to encircle his bulging bicep. Together, Cutter and she made the first cut of the cake. Lexie remembered eating a small piece and washing it down with a glass of water after Cutter confiscated her never-ending flute. That was her last recollection of her wedding night.

******

Cutter propped his new wife against wall with his right hand and swiped the key card with his left while the hotel bellman waited patiently with her luggage. Cutter guided her into the hotel suite that had been his temporary digs for the duration of his stay. She was standing on her own reasonably well, so he directed the hotel employee where to deposit the luggage, tipped him, bolted the door, and turned his attention to his bride. She was gone! Then he heard the water running in the bathroom sink, and relaxed. He had removed the tux jacket, his shoes, and was working on the studs of his shirt when she reappeared. A little wobbly still, she gave him a sheepish grin as she approached him.

"Cutter, would you help me? I can't seem to get out of this thing."

He was more than happy to play her lady's maid. She'd managed to unfasten the top four of the endless row of tiny buttons. What had held the promise of a little foreplay disrobing Lexie for the first time, turned into a frustrating task. "Christ! How did you get into this gown?"

"I had to step into it so I wouldn't mess my hair."

Okay, she is not operating at anything close to normal yet, he thought. "I was referring to the half million buttons."

"Mom fastened them."

Eve's smaller fingers probably made quick work of what he was finding a major undertaking. He supposed she would object if he just ripped the rest of them off to get to the enticing back being exposed in the painfully slow process. Finally, he completed the task.

"Thank you, I think I can manage from here."

He was going nuts waiting for her to remove her arm from the tight-fitting sleeve, so he retired to the bathroom to remove his shirt and clean up a bit. A shave wouldn't hurt either, he decided, running his hand over his chin. He returned filled with anticipation, but in much better control of his burgeoning lust to find his new wife passed out and sprawled across the bed. Her gown was still in her hand; the effort of working her way out of it must have wiped her out. Once more, he played her attendant and hung her gown in the garment bag with the dressmaker's logo on it.

Cutter talked to her, kissed the nape of her neck, and resorted to trying to shake her awake. Nothing. She didn't move a muscle. It brought back the scenes in the hospital when she was comatose and on life support. He consoled himself by working on the puzzle of undoing her hairdo and removing the woven string of beads. Loosening her braids gave him the pleasure of putting his fingers in her long silky hair. He picked her up to move her limp form to one side of the bed, pulled back the covers before moving her to the opposite side, and then covering her. He was not about to remove her slip or the lacy lingerie visible beneath. He wanted her, but he wanted her aware and participating. On his first night as a husband, he consoled himself with holding his new wife in his arms while they slept.

*****

The next morning, she was still dead to the world. "Come on, Lex, move it or we are going to miss the boat!" As was his habit, Cutter rose before dawn, showered, packed what he had brought with him, and ordered breakfast from room service to allow her to sleep it off. He informed her that breakfast had arrived, and this time punctuated it with a playful crack on her butt. That got a reaction; she came up swinging.

"Breakfast is here. But if you don't get a move on, you're not going to have time to eat it before we have to go."

Lexie sat up and tried to focus on the strange, rolling room. It didn't look familiar to her, but she assumed they'd spent the night here. Cutter was already dressed and working on a cup of coffee. Head thumping like an evil blacksmith was using her pickled brain for an anvil she walked softly across the carpet toward the bathroom to avoid aggravating it, or her rebelling stomach. She bypassed the food for the moment, gathered her overnight case, and clean undergarments.

"Remind me never to touch champagne in the future."

"You can count on it."

"Cutter, how should I dress? You never said what we were doing today."

"We're going for a boat ride, assuming we don't miss it."

By the time she got cleaned up and dressed, the bellman was there to collect their luggage. She stuffed the clothes she slept in into the zipper pocket on the front of the largest piece of luggage, gulped down her orange juice, took a couple of bites of cold eggs, and then decided to bypass them and the equally cold bacon. While Cutter was checking out, she spotted the complementary continental breakfast offerings. Lexie selected a couple of Danish cheese pastries on a napkin, filled a paper cup from the coffee dispenser, poured in three little containers of half and half, capped her cup, and rejoined Cutter.

The trip to Sandusky took a little over an hour and a half. The ibuprofen she'd taken once she'd unwrapped one of the glasses on the little tray in the bathroom was finally kicking in. Her stomach was easing, too, since she fed it. At first she was grateful for the blessed silence, but Cutter hadn't spoken to her since leaving the hotel. She wished she could remember last night, but her last clear image was of cutting the wedding cake. He was not a gabby sort of guy, and she knew he was a man of few words unless he was conducting business. Well, nothing ventured, nothing gained, Gram always said. "Cutter, do you know how to get to the boat dock?"

"I got good directions from the people who run the jet boat."

Okay, that didn't stimulate any conversation, she thought and decided to try again. "Are you disappointed? You're so quiet this morning."

"Disappointed in what, Lex?"

"Well, in last night. I assume that we, ah... you know?"

"You're going to have to be more specific. I have no idea what you are talking about." He knew very well what she was asking him, but after the frustrating night he had spent he was not inclined to ease her mind.

"Did we consummate our wedding vows?"

"Consummate?" He lost it, and actually laughed at her. "That sounds like your grandmother talking, Lex."

"Okay, so I was hammered. I don't remember anything after the damned wedding cake. Did we have sex?" He deliberately prolonged her anxiety. "You're not going to tell me. Are you, Cutter?"

"I'm concentrating on the road, and attempting to forget our less than memorable wedding night."

"That bad, huh?"

"About as disappointing as it could get, Lex."

"Well, I really don't have a lot of experience at that sort of thing. I am bound to get better with practice. Right?"

Thankfully, he had located the designated parking near the boat landing. Her questions about last night, and subsequent comments, were having uncomfortable physical effects on his male anatomy. She got out as soon as he parked the dark green Yukon that was now as familiar as his silver one back home. Lexie retrieved her overnight case, the small carry-on, and her larger pull-behind piece of luggage. She started off toward the boat dock, never looking back.

"Lex, do you want to take the garment bag, too?"

"No, leave it. Maybe someone will steal it, and I won't ever have to look at it again."

Okay, he figured that his tactics had backfired big-time. He had been goading her a bit about her lack of memory, but she took it as dissatisfaction with her performance in bed. She wouldn't even look at him since her cryptic remark concerning her wedding gown. Lexie continued to walk down the dock in the direction of the waiting watercraft while he checked their bags and picked up the prepaid tickets. She took the seat nearest the rail of the jet boat, and he hoped she wasn't planning on taking a swim as he sat in the seat next to her. Before they left the dock, a member of the crew gave them emergency instructions, including the location of life preservers. It was almost the same spiel the airline attendants gave before every flight.

Lexie was feeling pretty lousy; any help from the pills she had taken for her headache had now faded. Thankfully, the lake was calm, but she hugged close to the rail of the boat to catch a breeze and will her rebelling stomach to calm. She must have really made a fool of herself last night. Silent prayers battled with the incessant drumming in her head as she prayed she hadn't embarrassed Cutter in public. She was grateful that she had braided her hair when the jet express picked up speed.

The boat was filled to capacity on the crossing to Put-in-Bay. So Cutter made due with holding his wife's hand, now adorned with her new wedding band. He didn't want to attempt to smooth things over in public. She'd proved to be a bit unpredictable and could decide to attempt to brain him when he admitted the truth. He mulled it over and thought that perhaps it would be best not to even try.

*****

Several fleets of golf-carts were located near the boat landing, some complete with drivers who were the island version of a shuttle service. Others were rentals for tourists not inclined to walk the island. Room reservations had been made at the Put-in-Bay Resort. The place was relatively new, sporting a Caribbean theme. After they checked in and located their room, Lexie dug out a couple more tablets to relieve the increasing throbbing behind her tearing eyes.

Cutter was concerned. Lexie looked to be on the verge of tears. "Lex, I didn't intend to make light of your anxiety, or upset you. I wasn't in a position to have that conversation while trying to keep my attention on the unfamiliar roads."

"Don't worry about it, Cutter. I guess my excessive intake of Potter's expensive French bubbly is still working on me. Maybe we could have some lunch? I might feel better once the pills kick in and I get some real food in me."

The in-house restaurant offered a good selection of lunch entrées, and excellent iced tea. When she had her glass refilled their eyes connected, and both were thinking of the tea debacle that was the proverbial straw that broke her resolve to finish her bookkeeping commitment. Lexie was not excited about the prospect of returning to Texas, or having to deal with Maria again. The Decker threats only added to her stress level. She had hoped that what she and Cutter shared was a love strong enough to overcome the negatives, but one day of marriage and he was already disappointed with her.

Back in their room, Lexie sat at a small, faux walnut dressing table to undo her braid and brush her hair. When Cutter emerged from the bathroom—showered, shirtless, and barefoot—the silly signs that showed up every summer at home popped into her head: no shirt, no shoes, no service. His cell phone interrupted his forward progress. The call sounded like business, so she kicked off her shoes, settled in the middle of the oversized bed with her laptop, and proceeded to check her e-mail. She was deciding how to answer Mel's very personal inquiry about their wedding night when Cutter took the computer from her hands. He closed the lid and placed it across the room on a small round table, flanked on either side by a pair of rattan armchairs. About to give him a piece of her mind for his rude behavior, the words died unspoken when she noticed the heat in his eyes, and his predatory gait back toward the bed. Lexie was immobilized and instantly empathized with the deer frozen in the headlights of an oncoming truck and unable to escape the inevitable.

Lexie had been lamenting the cool weather, as she was unable to make use of the huge outdoor pool, but as soon as his lips took possession of hers, she had a feeling she was caught in an unprecedented Texas heat wave. He made quick work of her outer garments, lingering over her lacy bra and panties, the ones that her mother had insisted on purchasing. He then proceeded to scorch the bared intimate places they'd kept covered. I am going to burn every one of these skimpy lacy undergarments the first chance I get. As thoughts of destroying her intimate apparel flitted through her mind, her over-stimulated body arched up begging for more. Cutter was more than willing to accommodate her. Unbearable pressure began to build within her as he continued his onslaught. She was gasping for breath when he drove her over the edge. It felt like an internal earthquake shattered her, complete with tremors and aftershocks, as she gradually came back to reality again. She felt drained, like a boneless rag doll. She was just beginning to catch her breath when he returned, completely naked, and started working her up to a fever pitch once more.

It was the sharp, intense pain as he forced his entry that made her realize she was completely helpless and at his mercy. A bucket of ice water couldn't have put out her ardor any quicker than the strong pain now threatening to split her in two. She tried to push him off, but couldn't budge him. So she took a swing at his head. He captured her hands up over her head effectively gaining complete control. He didn't move. However, he kept her pinned beneath him. She tried to wiggle loose, but it only hurt more. "Get the hell off of me, Cutter!"

"Calm down, Lex. The pain will ease quicker if you relax and let your body adjust to mine."

"Like hell! I should have realized since the rest of you is so damn big, that would be too."

It was causing him a great deal of discomfort to go so slowly, but he hadn't expected his little bride to still be a virgin at the age of twenty-four! Fortunately, her body betrayed her brain and convulsed as it gloved his sex; he let instinct take over, joining her in an earth-shattering climax well worth his prolonged wait for her to catch up. Cutter rolled on to his back, taking her along with him and reversing their positions. They slept a while in the tangle of damp sheets. Then he woke her with his roving hands for an encore.

Lexie couldn't believe how achy, battered, and bruised she felt, inside and out, yet her out-of-control hormones responded once again with even more urgency. Not the slow easy process of their first mating, this time as he coached her in their reverse roles, she was the aggressor. She collapsed on his broad lightly furred chest, fighting for air and some return to sanity.

******

Lexie turned on the shower to wash away the sweat from her body, along with the evidence of their recent activity. Everywhere she touched with the soapy washcloth was tender, from her breasts to her lower body. She heard him call out.

"Lex, are you sure you don't need a hand?" He punctuated his question with another amused chuckle.

She had refused his previous offer to share the shower with her. His perverted suggestion to wash hers if she washed his, prompted her to reply that if he touched her again, she was filing for divorce, making theirs one of the shortest marriages in history. All he did was laugh at her threat, but he did agree not to invade her space in the bathroom "this time."

*****

She was grateful she hadn't given in to her attraction to Cutter back in the beginning; he would surely have thought she was a loose woman after his money. Lexie couldn't believe the things that they had done, and shared the past three days. She even relented on the showering alone stipulation of their first afternoon on the island. They shared meals out of the room, and walked the island, exploring the sites and points of interest. But the bulk of their brief honeymoon was spent exploring one another's bodies. Lexie discovered a whole new twist on the old shower routine. Who would have thought that a shower could amount to some very stimulating foreplay, or that it was possible to make love standing up, wet and lathered with soap, without serious injury to the bathing lovers? It was all a revelation.

Embarrassed might not be the correct word to describe her naïve inquiry about consummating their wedding night. She had no doubt that if she had an extreme case of amnesia her body would attest to what had happened, beginning with the afternoon of their arrival on South Bass Island and every time since. After a steamy morning shower, breakfast, and a walk to the unique lighthouse with attached living quarters that was now part of The Ohio State University, they returned to their honeymoon suite.

Lexie kicked off her shoes, sat cross-legged on the bed, and clicked on the TV. The lake looked really choppy when they had been out by the 1897 Queen Ann style structure attached to the fascinating old lighthouse. So, she decided to check the local forecast, but a national news story caught her attention. "Cutter. Come look at this!"

CHAPTER 5

DUE to the choppy lake conditions, the ferry transports were on stand-down until it calmed enough for a safe crossing. Undeterred, Cutter hired a charter pilot who was willing to fly them back to the mainland. Their honeymoon came to an abrupt end.

"I'll call you when I get back, Lex." She was soundly kissed in her living room, amidst her luggage, and in front of her puzzled Grandmother; he turned, closed the door behind him, and—poof—he was gone.

"What happened, Alexandra? We didn't expect you for a couple of more days."

"I will tell you later Gram. Right now, I need to carry this stuff upstairs, and then take a nap."

She also required some privacy to call Mel's father on the outside chance he hadn't caught the news that morning. Benson was on top of the situation and had already dispatched Booker to investigate the happenings at the Lazy K. Mr. Potter also mentioned the allegations in subsequent media coverage that one of the hands at the Rocking R had been arrested. No wonder Cutter had cut short their time together after checking in with Sam and Jim. Lexie burrowed under the quilt on her bed, closed her eyes, and prayed that the need for vengeance she shared with Mr. Potter and Booker wouldn't somehow land in Cutter's lap.

Familiar musical tones woke her a few hours later. Still combating the residual fog of sleep, she fumbled for her phone. Too late! It was Cutter; she checked the messages and called him back. Strange, she didn't remember a hand named Pete. but she didn't know the names of most of the ranch hands. However, mentally going over payroll names she could not remember a Pete or Peter. Cutter had just arrived back at the ranch, and was on his way to try to bail out his employee. She was in the process of disconnecting from her new husband for the second time that day when her Mom came into her room to wake her for the evening meal.

Dinner was more like an interrogation than a family meal. Mom started it all off by demanding to know why she was home so early, and alone.

"I was checking on the weather when a story came on about a fire at the Lazy K that was the suspected starting point of a spreading wildfire. It was reported that someone had been arrested on suspicion of arson. Cutter called home to verify what we'd seen and heard on the news. The suspect in custody was one of his ranch hands. We couldn't get off the island by jet express or the traditional ferry, so Cutter hired one of the pilots that make that run all winter. He dropped me off here, and caught a plane back to Texas."

"Why didn't you go with him?"

How was she supposed to answer that? Mom already knew about the Skip versus Maria thing, although she didn't know about the other points of their premarital agreement. "Well, mostly because he didn't ask me, but I think he was honoring our agreement about Skip. He was in a big hurry to get back, and there wasn't time to make arrangements for my dog to go along."

Grandma was scowling at both of them. "What kind of agreement did you make with that man?"

Gram was obviously offended she'd been left out of some privileged information that would be prime gossip at one of her Senior Citizen functions. Lexie figured it wouldn't matter much now, so she told her the story of Maria.

"Alexandra! You mean you agreed to let him retain that spiteful woman so that you could take your dog?"

"Don't worry, Gram, if she gets out of line again, Skip can have what's left of her for a chew toy after I finish with her."

Mom was scrutinizing her while she embellished on her nemesis at the Rocking R. Her rendition for the benefit of her grandmother's injured sensibilities appeared less comprehensive than the version she'd heard. Eve was unable to shake the feeling that her daughter was still hiding something. "Lexie, you wouldn't know anything about Booker's unexpected assignment, would you?"

Lexie hated to lie to her mom, but she couldn't say much. She was a trusted co-conspirator; the less other people knew at this point the better. "Really, Mom, how would I know what Booker is up to? I only got back this afternoon." She escaped further questioning by taking Skip for a walk and promising to clean up the kitchen when she returned.

Lexie mulled over her options while she walked with Skip. Tomorrow was Friday. By Monday, she would be heading to the Texas panhandle. First thing in the morning she would call her vet to see if Skip needed a health certificate and proof of inoculations for the trip. At the very least she would need Skip's records for his future vet. She should also drop off her Suburban for a check up before packing it with her belongings. She didn't have a GPS in her vehicle; it was not state of the art like Mel's ill-fated Escalade had been. She did have a good road atlas, her iPhone, and her Suburban had a hookup for her laptop. All that and unexpected detours aside, the trip shouldn't take more than three or four days. She didn't think she would ever forget the ill-fated trip to find Mel's dotcom Mr. Right, and she prayed this trip would have a better outcome.

Saturday morning the packing chore began. She decided to take all of her underwear including the lacy stuff from her honeymoon that she'd decided to hold on to a bit longer. Clothing was sorted into what she wanted to keep, and what could be donated to Goodwill. Lexie kept some of her winter things, at Cutter's suggestion. "Be sure to bring your winter clothing, Lex. We can get some really nasty winter weather."

She'd waited for the punch line, but he had seemed completely serious, so she did a little online research. It looked like her new address was located in the land of extremes.

Grandma's calico quilt, like Skip, would not be left behind. Her next trip was down to the basement to retrieve her saddle and load it. She was assessing her packing job and rearranging some things to make room for her humongous tack trunk when Mom pulled her little red Focus up behind Lexie's two-toned black and silver, larger vehicle. Eve was wearing a skirt and blazer and had obviously put in a half day at work. "What are you doing, Lexie?"

"Repacking to make room for my tack trunk. I forgot how huge it was until I saw it when I brought the saddle up."

"Give me a chance to change into some old slacks, and I will help you lug it up the stairs."

Lexie and her mom slid the trunk up the basement stairs, out the back door, and up to her suburban, which made it only necessary to lift the backbreaker once. After a lunch, she found herself reshuffling her belongings, one more time, so her small bag and her overnight case were easy to get at. She placed her mom's luggage in the back seat. Gram took one look at the packed vehicle, and declined their invitation to make the trip with them.

Mom took a week of her annual two-week vacation to accompany her on the trip. It appeared that her new husband and her mother didn't want her traveling alone. Together they'd worked out a plan for Mom to ride with her and fly back. Lexie didn't blame Grandma for not wanting to take the long ride in the now cramped vehicle. Mom's luggage didn't take up much room in the second seat—it consisted of a makeup case, small carry-on, and one bag to check on her way home—but Skip would easily take up the remainder of the space.

The decision was unanimous to depart Sunday, following mass and breakfast. Their strategy was to avoid the Monday morning rush hour on the Interstate.

"I think we should call it an early night, Lexie. We can make an earlier service and be on the road by ten. All that remains is for you to pack your dog and his bowls."

That evening, when she talked to Cutter he attempted to convince her to wait a couple of more days.

"Cutter, Mom already took a week of her vacation time beginning Monday. If we don't leave in the morning, Skip and I will have to make the trip alone."

He relented. She understood his concern with the outbreaks of wildfires in the neighboring drought-ridden states. Her new husband was worried about the potential for them to be caught in one of the lightning-ignited fires. A huge area of the state and neighboring Oklahoma had been subjected to a large number of lightning strikes, but the dark clouds kept rolling on by without spitting out enough moisture to make a difference. The fast moving front brought heavy winds that fanned the fires and spawned dust storms—not the heavy, hundred-mile storms that had just blanketed the greater Phoenix area or the one that had hit them in Lubbock not long after Lexie had left for Ohio—but bad enough to foul the dwindling water supply.

Cutter thanked God those winds hadn't kicked up when the Lazy K went up in flames, or the Rocking R would have most likely been a pile of burnt ash, too. Not much was left of Sophie's old place, but at least Pete was in the clear. Sam had put him to work watering the horses and throwing each of them a couple of slabs of hay. Two of the younger hands were pulling bales from the hay barn for him, and the others gave Pete an alibi for the afternoon of the fire. What little Cutter was able to find out from the sheriff's office amounted to the fire appeared to be arson, and then he was referred to the chief of their small volunteer fire department for updates. He was able to get confirmation that the fire was deliberately set. The process was frustrating, and he knew there was more to this, but information was scarce. Unknown to him, Booker had arrived on a flight soon after the one that had brought him home.

Booker teamed up with Patrick Boyd as soon as his plane touched down in Lubbock. They'd discovered the fire had been set to cover up a murder. Shell casings from automatic weapons were in abundance around the perimeter of the house. Forensics had the remains of the crispy critter recovered from the rubble. All they had been able to determine so far was that the victim was a male thirty-five to forty, and had been shot multiple times prior to the fire. Booker hoped the dead man wasn't Decker; he wanted the pleasure of beating him to within an inch of his miserable life.

******

Mrs. Parker and the new Mrs. Ross arrived at the Rocking R on Wednesday afternoon. The trip was uneventful; they'd had to locate lodging each night at a motel that welcomed Skip, but it wasn't a major problem. They had stopped periodically for some sightseeing and to walk the dog. Eve's penchant for shopping was squelched by the lack of space in their transport vehicle. Rain showers that turned into a major cloudburst by the time they drove onto the Rocking R greeted the pair of travelers.

Lexie knew the rain was much needed, but memories of the floodwaters back in June flashed through her mind and brought on a spontaneous outbreak of goose bumps. She drove close to the mudroom entrance of the house. Mother and daughter made a dash through the downpour, after quickly unloading only their overnight cases and small carry-on bags. Lexie managed to latch on to the towel they had used to wipe Skip's paws dry before he reentered the vehicle from exercise or relief stops. She quickly fired off a few covert commands to Skip, "Komm hier bitte, mein Freund. Bleib!" They set the sparse luggage on the floor, kicked off their muddy shoes, and Lexie began working to dry off Skip.

She knew Maria was not around when the cook failed to show up before she finished wiping her dog's paws clean. They picked up their footwear and proceeded through the kitchen to the main hall. Cutter had suggested putting her mom in the room she herself had occupied a few months earlier. "What a lovely room, Lexie."

"I liked it." After she unpacked her blow dryer and completed drying her canine companion, she dialed Cutter's cell. Lexie closed the bedroom door and plopped on the large bed next to her already reclining mother. "Hi, cowboy! I thought I would let you know we've arrived at the ranch. Thank God Maria wasn't here when we came in through the mudroom. It took me a good fifteen minutes to get the mud toweled off of Skip."

When their conversation ended, she noticed that her mother had already zonked off, and Skip was stretched out on the floor at the foot of the bed, having doggie dreams. Lexie thought they had the right idea. She closed her eyes and joined them for the impromptu nap.

That was the way Cutter found them a few hours later when he returned home. The only one who stirred was the dog. Skip decided the intruder wasn't a threat and resumed his snooze. Cutter showered, shaved off a three-day growth of stubble, and then checked on the sleeping trio after he dressed. He decided to let them sleep while he unloaded the suburban—all but the large trunk, stuffed with tack, and a stock saddle. Those items would end up occupying space in one of the tack rooms in the horse barn. Lexie needed the rest. He didn't plan on either of them getting much sleep that night.

******

Maria had been on her best behavior since their arrival on Wednesday, but Lexie noticed her glaring at Skip when he accompanied her to dinner and took up his customary spot on the floor near her seat at the dining table. Skip didn't trust the cook anymore than she did, or maybe he just sensed his mistress's dislike of the woman. He kept a watchful eye on her, and if she ventured too close he curled his lip while his black and tan coat stood up along his ruff. Lexie set his bowls up in the office where she would be spending several hours each day. She kept him with her during the waking hours, but night he slept with her mother in the adjoining room. He'd become a little upset by Cutter and Lexie's exuberant reunion. It was her husband's suggestion that Skip should keep Mom company while she was visiting, so the dog wouldn't bite off any vital parts of his anatomy.

Mother and Daughter piled into the Suburban once more to go on a shopping trip to Lubbock Thursday morning. Skip enjoyed the ride with his head sticking out the second seat window. Lexie patted her dog's head, "Skip, Schütz das auto!" While Mom was busy checking out the clearance racks, Skip stood guard over the vehicle. He let anyone who ventured too near know that he was a force to be reckoned with. Lexie could have left the keys in the ignition even with all the windows open to their fullest, no one in their right mind would challenge the hundred and eight pound canine. Lexie took a few selections into the fitting room, but never tried them on. Instead, she used the privacy provided to touch base with Booker.

"Are you about ready to wind this up, Mom? I need to check on Skip, and we have a lunch date."

"Let me try on these jeans, and then we can go."

Cutter's offer to take them on a horseback tour of some of the ranch had facilitated today's unplanned buying binge. Mom hadn't packed anything appropriate for horseback travel. Lunch went well, considering the topic of the fire at the Lazy K. To say that her mother was delighted to see Booker would have been a gross understatement, and it was obvious that he was as pleased as she at the unexpected encounter. The older couple seemed enchanted; their eyes clashed often radiating heat that made Lexie wonder what she had missed while she was at Put-in-Bay with her new husband. She decided to excuse herself to allow them some privacy. She would have to wait to confer with Booker by phone on the more closely held information he'd uncovered.

"I think I'll check on Skip and run over to the bank. It shouldn't take more than twenty minutes. Enjoy the rest of your lunch. When I get back, Mom, we can find you a pair of boots to go with your new cowgirl outfit."

Booker was gone when she returned to the table, and he had picked up the tab. In her whopping twenty-four years, she could never remember her mother making such quick work choosing footwear! On the return trip, Eve admitted she had a dinner date for that evening.

"You have a date with Booker?" Lexie couldn't help the little girl giggle that bubbled out. "Who would have guessed?"

"What's so funny?'

"Not a thing. I was surprised a bit, that's all. I think it's great."

*****

Booker showed up at the Rocking R as Maria was about to serve dinner. The departing couple became the topic of the meal conversation. Jim jumped on the topic. "Cutter, did you know he was in the area?"

He shook his head in response, but was suspicious about his wife's lack of curiosity. She was busy carving the steak on her plate and refused to make eye contact with him. Every bite she took was punctuated by the plop of another piece of steak on the floor; it was quickly sucked up by the big furry vacuum cleaner parked at her feet. He also noticed Maria scowl every time Lexie dropped a morsel for Skip.

"I don't know, Cutter. I heard that Boyd had teamed up with some big, mean-looking, Yankee over at the Lazy K, but no one is talking about the aftermath of the fire over there."

Lexie's interest in the fire at what used to be Decker's place was as lacking as her usually opinionated take on a variety of subjects.

"Lex, did you know Booker was here?"

How was she supposed to answer that without lying? " Yes. Mom and I had lunch with him this afternoon."

"And the two of you merely happened to run into him?"

"Sort of." She shot him a silent plea to drop the subject that he didn't miss, but she knew he was only biding his time until they were alone.

Cutter caught her off guard when he suggested she change into something more appropriate for riding and meet him in the horse barn. By the time she entered the aisle of the double stall row, Cutter and Sam had a big dappled gray gelding tacked up with her saddle, but she didn't see his big black anywhere.

"Sam and I picked out a couple of horses that you can try for yourself and your mom."

With all the stress related to Booker's activities, and the pending interrogation by Cutter, she had forgotten about the planned ride for tomorrow. Unlike Booker, who wanted the pleasure of putting his lethal hands on David Decker, she hoped the dead man found at the ranch was him. It would relieve a lot of stress on her part, and it would permanently put Mel out of his reach.

Out of habit she checked her girth and made sure her stirrups were adjusted and securely fastened. The bridle was not one of hers, so she opened the gelding's mouth to check the bit he was carrying. Satisfied, Lexie followed Sam into a large covered arena. She didn't know what she had expected, but a thoroughly modern, immaculately kept, stable and work arena was a pleasant surprise. Sam was standing by the horse's head, waiting for her to mount. "Okay, Sam what's wrong with him?'

"Nothing, Lexie. He is a good solid ranch horse."

"Then why are you standing at his head like he's a green colt, or a loco bronc?"

"I figured to give you a hand while Cutter gave you a leg up. He is a bit of a climb up for a little girl."

"Really? Who usually rides him?"

"He is one of Cutter's personal ranch string."

Lexie looked at her husband and asked for the horse's name. "Blue."

Okay, not very original. She made a mental note not to let Cutter name anything of importance, like any children they might have. She relieved Sam of the reins and led Blue to the center of the arena. She checked the girth again; he hadn't blown up holding air, so the girth didn't need any further adjustment.

Cutter watched his little wife mount the sixteen-one-hand gelding and was amazed how easy she made the long stretch up to the stirrup look. She started Blue off at a walk, turning him in small circles one way, then the other; Cutter knew she was getting the feel of his gelding, and he was impressed. She stopped him, backed him a few steps, and then repeated the process at a trot. He watched Lexie move him into a lope circling half the arena to the right several times; she came through the middle of the sand-based work area and executed a flaw-less lead change before circling to the left. Suddenly, she rolled him back and took off down the far end of the arena where she sat down deep and slid him to a stop! Then she repeated the process in the opposite direction. Blue appeared to be enjoying himself; he really went to ground on the second stop, and spun like a top when she asked him. The big guy was a little worked up following the spins, but she made him stand for a few min-utes then walked him around the perimeter of the arena several times before dismounting, loosening his girth, and returning his reins to Sam.

"He is fine for me on the ride tomorrow, but I think some-thing smaller and less intimidating for Mom."

Occupied with getting to know Blue, she hadn't noticed the old man conversing with Cutter when he had entered the work arena. Cutter introduced him as Pete Miller. So this is Pete, she thought.

Sam brought out a little smaller sorrel gelding with a huge blaze that threatened to make him a bald faced horse; he also had two hind socks. His name, of course, was Blaze. She went through the whole process with Blaze, but unlike Blue, he qui-etly went about his business. Lexie bumped him a few times with her legs, bounced on this back, and either pitched his reins way too loose, or grabbed the lines in a death grip while traveling at a trot. Lexie tried all the mistakes an inexperi-enced rider could make that came to mind. He took it all in stride, humoring her like she must be slightly loony. She tried another bay gelding, and a seal-brown mare. Both were really nice horses, but she decided on Blaze for Mom, and opted for Blue for herself. Her biggest concern was getting a saddle with short enough stirrups for her mother. Sam assured her he had an old saddle that he'd cleaned up specifically for her mother's use.

Lexie wasn't anybody's fool. She knew Cutter had used the selection of horses as a ruse to distract her from the coming confrontation about Booker's presence here on the heels of the fire at the Lazy K. He and Sam had already made the selection of Blue and Blaze before she ever got there. It wouldn't have been so obvious if they had thrown the other two horses in between them, but she played along. She would probably pay for it tomorrow; it had been months since she had last spent any time on a horse. Her husband joining her in the shower interrupted her thought process. It looked like he had more distractions in mind.

The shower, as usual, turned into some very stimulating foreplay. They ended up toweling each other off before Cutter cut the sexual stimulation short by carrying her to the bed, not bothering to close the bathroom door. Lexie was grateful her mother was not home at the moment, and that Skip was closed in down the hall in the office eating his doggy dinner. She was anything but quiet and her body quaked to fulfillment almost immediately.

It didn't take long for round two. Somewhere in the next couple of hours, she did get up to use the bathroom, check on Skip, and drink a big glass of tea. The witching hour had passed, and Mom was still not home. Poor Cutter must be exhausted; he didn't stir when she left the bed or returned. Skip returned with her and curled up on the floor in his usual spot at the foot of the bed.

She snuggled up next to her sleeping husband and let her fingers roam his chest and abs, gradually working her hand lower. She almost had a heart attack when his male appendage grew before her eyes and stood at attention. Lexie was amazed at his response to her touch! He had a completely satisfied grin on his too-attractive male countenance. He returned her tentative exploration with a lot more confidence than she'd displayed. She thought she was going to die from wanting when he began to lower her hips toward her ultimate prize. Cutter was making a super human effort to take it slow and easy, but she didn't want slow she wanted fulfillment. Lexie gasped at the pain as she impaled herself on his raised sword of love, but even the pain didn't deter her from her frantic quest. Somewhere in the back of her mind it occurred to her as she collapsed on his chest that he had been holding back up until that point, most likely because of their size disparity.

"Lex, are you alright?" No answer. She was sound asleep. Cutter smiled as he faded into a blissful sleep. Unless he was mistaken, which he doubted, he would be a father by the end of May. Neither of them was aware of what time Eve returned home. Predawn Cutter took full advantage of his wife's need for her mate while she plowed furrows in his back with her nails. He was a happy man, but he wondered if his little wife had any idea what had just happened. He'd spent his life breeding and raising animals. When a mare's or a heifer's height of estrus was reached, even the most reluctant of them broke down and sought what the stallion or bull had to offer. It was obvious to him that his little wife had just reached those heights on a human level, and it was well worth the slightly painful scratches on his back.

Cutter let her sleep while he went about his morning chores, but he intended to follow up enthusiastically over the next few days to ensure the Ross line.

CHAPTER 6

THE morning ride went off without a hitch. Lexie and Blue had hit it off the day before, and things only improved from there. Eve and Blaze got along well too. Mom was a decent rider; Lexie had forgotten that when she was a small child, it had been her mom who used to take her horseback riding. She said it was something she'd done on her short honeymoon with Lexie's dad, and had enjoyed the experience immensely. Skip enjoyed the outing as much as everyone else and he tagged along beside Blue.

Lexie was glad she was bringing up the rear with Skip, for most of the ride, and that Cutter had stationed himself next to her mom. They were busy yackety-yacking. She overheard Booker mentioned in the conversation several times, and dropped Blue back a little more each time that his name came up. She was hoping not to be drawn in to the conversation. Lexie had expected to be stiff or sore from riding the evening before, but her muscles loosened up the first half hour back in the saddle. What she didn't expect was the irritation and arousal between her legs that had nothing whatsoever to do with riding. By the time they returned to the barn, she was wet and throbbing. Mom saved her a major embarrassment by making an excuse to find a bathroom. She handed her horse off to Pete as her mother had to Sam, and accompanied her mom to the house.

While Eve took first dibs on the john, Lexie changed her jeans and underwear. She was mortified to find the wetness had penetrated her undies and her jeans; she prayed the suede seat on her new reining saddle wasn't sporting a corresponding telltale wet spot. A quick change and opting for her running shoes rather than the boots she'd been wearing, she entered the bathroom as soon as her mother finished. Cleaned up and relatively composed Lexie walked down to the dining room for lunch along with her mother.

Things went downhill beginning with lunch. Cutter offered to drive Mom to the airport in the morning. Booker had changed his flight back to match hers, and he would be picking her up in the morning.

"Really, Cutter, you and Lexie won't have to drive me to Lubbock and then make the return-trip using up most of your morning. Booker has the rental to drop off at the airport anyway."

He was addressing Eve but was giving Lexie an accusatory stare when he asked her mother, "Then he's completed his mysterious mission here?"

"I don't know, Cutter. He's been very vague about the reason for suddenly flying to Lubbock. Like I told you on the ride, Lexie probably knows more about what he's been up to than I do. However, she was very evasive on our trip here, and I haven't been able to talk with her since she set up the lunch meeting with him yesterday."

Cutter filed away the fact his wife had initiated contact with Booker while she deliberately neglected to notify her husband of her plans for the day until she was well off of the ranch.

Lexie was concentrating on her enchilada and thinking, jeez, thanks a lot, Mom. She was really beginning to hate the constant Tex-Mex meals that Maria served most of the time. Lexie had only been picking at her lunch. At that moment, Cutter told her mom not to worry that he and Lex would find a way to occupy their morning; what little she had ingested was making an attempt to crawl its way out.

"We may even take another morning ride once we see you and Booker on your way." His suggestion felt more like a threat than an invitation. She intuitively knew that he was holding off on their showdown about Booker's activities until Mom was safely on her way home.

Lexie and Skip retreated to the sanctuary offered by her mother's temporary room. Maria wouldn't breach the connecting room while her mother was here, and she felt fairly confident that Cutter would honor their privacy. It was a little tricky trying to pack her mom's new riding boots into her already stuffed luggage. "Mom, why don't you let me ship them and your new cowgirl outfit home for you? Instead of trying to stuff them in the bag."

"I really should wash them, and a few other things, before packing them."

"Okay, I'll gather the clothes I want to wash, and we'll hit the laundromat in Lubbock. We can also have dinner out. I don't think I my stomach will stand another jalapeno-laced meal tonight."

Eve laughed at her daughter's description of Maria's culinary skills. "I know what you mean. The first day it was a treat, but it gets old really fast. I think I blew any chance I had with Booker; I ate like a glutton or a starving person last night."

Lexie gathered her laundry while she continued the conversation, reassuring her mom that having a good appetite was not going to lower her in Booker's eyes. Lexie picked up her shoulder bag, and glanced over at her dog, he was wagging his tail in anticipation. She couldn't take him along this time, but she didn't want to lock him in the office or the bedroom for hours. He had struck up a tail-wagging relationship with Sam, so she asked the horse manager if he would mind keeping Skip with him while they took care of a few errands in Lubbock. Sam was happy to have the dog for company. However, Cutter was anything but happy when she called him from the laundromat to inform him that she and her mom were going to eat at one of the local restaurants and would not be home for dinner.

"Is something wrong, Lexie?"

"Not really. I think Cutter is pissed at me. He thinks I'm avoiding him."

"Are you?"

"Yes."

They broke out in spontaneous laughter, stowed the clean laundry in the backseat, and went in search of a good meal. It was close to nine by the time they turned into the drive near the front of the house, and the night was as black as pitch with not a sign of stars or moonlight. The only illumination once she cut the headlights was the glow from the inside light sources.

Skip met them at the front door. He was loose and had the run of the house! Thankfully, Maria had gone home after cleaning up the kitchen. Cutter must have retrieved Skip from Sam's care. She followed her mom down the hall and was helping her to pack her now clean clothes. They'd shipped her boots and what they jokingly referred to as her cowgirl outfit, and two handbags she'd spotted in a leather goods store window on their afternoon outing. The box would be delivered in three to five business days.

A distant rumble of thunder punctuated Cutter's knock on the bedroom door; he pushed it open, leaned against the doorframe, and observed the scene before him. Lexie noted his hair was wet; his green plaid shirt was un-tucked and only half buttoned. Her new husband held a heavy bottomed highball glass half full of an amber-colored liquid. Most likely scotch she thought. That was his poison of preference, if memory served her. She wondered how much he had already imbibed of the potent brew.

She couldn't procrastinate much longer. Mom had an early flight the next morning and needed her sleep. Lexie gathered up her clean folded laundry, kissed her mother's cheek, and exited the blocked door. Cutter stood aside to let her pass then effectively blocked Skip. "Stay with Eve," he all but growled. His tone alone didn't bode well for the rest of the evening. She'd hoped he would postpone the inevitable brawl until her mom was gone.

Cutter had been struggling to control his temper; he didn't want a knock-down drag-out with her mother here, either. He watched his wife put her laundry away, which was a particularly sore spot with him—there were adequate laundry facilities here at home. She completely ignored him on her way to bathroom. The sounds of the shower, and then her hairdryer played on his frayed nerves. Aggravated by what he felt were more stalling tactics, he occupied himself by returning to the small bar in the front office and pouring a good three fingers of scotch in his seemingly bottomless glass. He wondered if his mother had been this frustrating and that was the reason his father had taken to drink.

She was sitting cross-legged on the bed brushing her hair when he returned, and an urge to run his hands through her silky blonde locks assailed him. Disgusted with his obsession where his new wife was concerned, he drained the remainder of the contents in the tumbler, and then set it on the nightstand with enough force to crack the thick glassware.

"Cutter, are you drunk?"

She stood up, placed her hairbrush on the dresser, and then turned to face him. "What is the matter with you tonight? Why did you feel the need to get shit-faced?"

She continued to stand there with her hands on her hips and stare at him like she was completely appalled.

"I'm not drunk yet, and unlike my hammered bride on our wedding night, I am a long way from being comatose."

"So, this is payback for some perceived slight?"

"Yeah, something like that. Also the fact that you take off without a word to anyone, even me."

"Well, the hell with you! I don't have to put up with your stinking mood, or your liquor-induced insults! I also don't need your permission to go to town or anywhere else."

She turned toward the door, intending to leave before her temper got the better of her, when like lightning he moved to scoop her up from behind, throwing her on the bed. Lexie moved nearly as fast as she sprung to her feet to deliver a well-placed uppercut to his solar plexus. The blow temporally doubled him up. The punch also sent a staggering pain shooting up her right arm. Again she made for the door, but she had been hampered by her position on the bed and not able to deliver a strong enough blow to keep him down the length of time required to make her escape. He made a grab for her, shredding her new blue negligee. This time when he tossed her on the bed she was naked, and he followed her down pinning her beneath his superior weight while he glared at her like he wanted to strangle her. Instead, he kissed her neck and shoulders working his way down her stiff, resistant body. He was not the gentle lover of the recent past.

This was way too rough and angry to be called foreplay of any kind, and she refused to cooperate, but Cutter knew how to manipulate her body until it betrayed her. Lexie was completely unable to control the physical response, even with the pain shooting through her wrist and lower arm. He was grinning now, because he had her at his mercy. It was hard to say which of them she hated most at that moment, Cutter or herself. He knew she would not scream at him with her mother and Skip in the adjoining room.

Lexie sobbed silently with the intensity and humiliation of her unwelcome response. Once the quake was over, she went limp but continued to experience aftershocks. She realized he had removed his weight from her body, but as she scanned the room through her waterlogged vision, she saw him remove his jeans and briefs. She tried to communicate to her traitorous limbs to kick out at him as he approached her again, but he had no difficulty getting her to comply with his instant replay. He applied his expert knowledge of his partner's anatomy until she shattered.

It appeared he was finished harassing her for the night. He climbed back into his jeans, not bothering with his briefs, picked up the cracked tumbler, and left the room closing the door behind him. Lexie tried in vain to make sense of what had just happened. She cried herself to sleep, her right arm adding to her overall misery.

His frustration with her evasiveness, and the drinking while waiting for her to decide to return, had messed with his better judgment. His temper had gotten the better of him and he had forgotten about her martial arts abilities. If she'd been on solid ground instead of trying to balance on the bed, he would probably still be out for the count. He absently rubbed his bruised upper abdomen. Last night she clawed up his back in a bout of passion, and twenty-four hours later she tried to put his lights out—not that he didn't have it coming. He got up from his leather chair and filled a new glass with more of the dog that bit him. After a few more drinks, he began to doze off in his chair. The sound of the breaking glass jarred him from his stupor. The new replacement tumbler had slipped from his relaxed fingers, and now decorated the hard surface of the office floor. Cutter retrieved the broom from the utility closet in the hall near the kitchen and dumped the pieces of the ill-fated tumbler into the office wastebasket to join its cracked predecessor. He decided to sleep the remainder of the night in the bunkhouse. He needed to put some distance between them before he did something he would regret even more than their recent encounter.

Cutter closed the front door and headed for one of the bunks usually reserved for the single ranch hands. He was in desperate need of a few hours' sleep and a clear head before he tackled her involvement with the mess over at the Lazy K. She had lied to him about the lunch date with Booker and he knew that she was lying by omission about her knowledge of events at the neighboring ranch. That discussion would have to wait until morning; he wasn't in any condition to ward off an attack if she was still bent on revenge for his behavior.

Lexie woke to the sounds of Skip's excited barking the following morning. She winced while slipping her right arm into a white terry robe to check on Skip. She went by way of the connecting bath. Mom was already packed and closing her makeup case.

Mom's "Good morning, sleepy head," was way too cheerful for Lexie's mood this morning.

"What's the matter with Skip, Mom?"

"Oh, poor puppy, he got all excited when I moved my luggage to the front door. I think he's under the impression that we are all going home."

"Maybe I shouldn't have brought him here? He would be better off at home with you and Grandma.

"Why didn't you wake me?"

She giggled! Her mother actually giggled. "Cutter said you had a long hard night and to let you sleep in."

"He ought to know. And of course, like everyone else around here, you do whatever Cutter says."

"What's wrong, Lexie? You're in a strange mood this morning."

" Give me a couple of minutes, Mom. I need to get cleaned up. I feel disgusting. Like a street walker."

Eve was worried. Lexie's attitude was not that of a happy newlywed. She hoped Lexie's grandmother hadn't exuded too much influence on how her daughter perceived men. Maybe she should have remarried, but she had never found the right man. Her daughter had been raised in a house full of women. Now she was part of a male dominated society. By the time

Lexie made her entry to the kitchen, Booker was already loading Eve's luggage She had hoped to talk with her daughter before departing.

Lexie was severely depressed that morning. She couldn't find the silver lining to the dark clouds following the storm of the night before. She battled impending tears while holding onto Skip's collar with her left hand as she said farewell to her mother. Booker and Cutter were having a conversation on the opposite side of the red Durango rental. She leaned in to kiss her mother's cheek one more time and spoke to her slightly above a whisper. "Please Mom, talk to Grandma about Skip. I think he will be better off back home. If she agrees, I'll make arrangements to send him home with the Williams boys the next time they make a hay delivery. Unless I decide to take him home myself before then."

Cutter was discussing the ownership of some Hereford-Longhorn crosses on Rocking R property belonging to the Lazy K outfit. Booker agreed to look into the situation, but he was as evasive as Cutter's new wife about the goings-on over there. He was close enough to hear part of Lexie's hushed conversation with her mother. Drinking to excess was one of the most stupid stunts he had pulled since his freshman year at A& M. Once the rental and its occupants were well out of sight, Lex collapsed on the lowest porch step with her arms around her dog, and her head buried in his coat. In hindsight, he should have brought them home with him, even if it took an extra day or two. Maybe their morning ride would distract her from the departure of her mother. He also figured the ride would give him the opportunity to talk with her and apologize for the previous night. At the same time, he hoped to gain some insight into Booker's involvement with Lexie and the connection she had with the events at Lazy K.

He was at a loss. How was he supposed to deal with her? She was obviously still upset. As he approached her, she lifted mistrustful, tearstained eyes in his direction. "Are you ready for our morning ride, Lex?"

"I really don't feel up to it this morning."

"Well, I reckon we can find something else to do this morning. I'm kind of beat myself. We could take a long nap or whatever, instead." She jumped up like someone had scalded her, mumbling about going in to put her boots on. "I'll take Skip with me, and saddle up the horses while you get ready."

She didn't even acknowledge him; like a wraith, she faded into the house. He saddled Blue for her then brought Rowdy out. Both horses were tacked up, and ready to begin their day when she finally showed up. Lexie was dressed much like the day before with a navy ball cap as head protection, jeans, a print western shirt, and rough-out boots, but this morning she'd also added a denim jacket. The addition of the jacket seemed out of place; it had been cooler yesterday morning, and neither of the women had bothered with a jacket. She took up Blue's reins and looked around.

"Where's Skip, Cutter?"

"He's spending the day with Sam. It wouldn't be a good idea to take him where we're going."

She didn't argue or even question where they were going. He figured she didn't care as long as she had some space to maneuver should he get aggressive. She lagged a good horse length behind Rowdy, and whenever he slowed his stallion for her to catch up, she slowed Blue keeping the distance between them.

The next two hours passed in a like manner. To say his wife was avoiding him would have been an extreme understatement.

He'd intended to prepare her for the sight of the emaciated herd being quarantined on the eastern border of the ranch, but her refusal to even get near enough for a conversation made that courtesy impossible.

Lexie was making the best of a painful ride. Her right wrist and arm were on fire. Fortunately, Blue guided well from leg and seat cues, and all he had to do was follow the horse in front of him. It was awkward attempting support her right arm with her left while trying to guide her horse with that lone functioning hand. Her future looked as bleak as the sepia landscape that stretched as far as the eye could see. Ink spots appeared before her eyes. At first she thought the spotty vision was due to gazing into the rising sun, or possibly the full force of pain working on her. The ibuprofen she'd taken before leaving was well worn off, but the spots grew larger. Soon they took on the forms of cattle and a couple of horsemen.

Her already queasy insides pitched, and bile rose as the pathetic cows came in to view. Every bone was visible on many, while others looked a little better, but hipbones, shoulders, and spinal columns were still prominent. A Rocking R stock truck pulled up as they approached. Three men she didn't know lowered a ramp, and began to push, pull, and prod five more skeletons covered in cowhide down the ramp to join the rest of the herd. Lexie didn't know any more about beef cattle now than she did in June when she almost ran over one of them on the road, but these looked a lot different to her. It was more than their sad condition. To her they appeared to be another breed.

The reason for this morning's torture became apparent to her when they rode close enough to see the Lazy K brand on their hips. Her sadist husband must think the shock value of the scene would loosen her tongue about what she knew of the status of their nearest neighbor to the east, but it wasn't her story to tell.

CHAPTER 7

The endless tears were eroding her naïve optimism regarding the longevity of marital bliss and were bound to leave deep grooves in her face. She really thought they had something special and their love could withstand life's roadblocks. Pathetic starving cattle weren't enough for Cutter. Oh, no. He had a point to make, so they rode on to the Lazy K.

Lexie had seen the photos of the dead and nearly dead cattle taken at the dry riverbed, but seeing them for real was more than she could handle. The bleached bones of the small calves were the worst. Before she could lose whatever was left in her stomach, she wheeled Blue a hundred and eighty degrees sand took off the way they had come. Cutter tried to explain to her about how he came upon the river of bones, but she'd already reached well beyond her threshold for abuse, both mental and physical. Her ears were deaf to his excuses for the latest assault on her. Jim and Pete's delivery of a pickup load of hay for the emaciated herd delayed Cutter while his wife kept going. Lexie made excellent use of her head start and Blue's ground-eating gallop. Every stride shot pain up her right arm and penetrated every fiber of her being.

Lexie dismounted; more aptly, she nearly fell from her horse. She avoided disaster by latching on to the saddle horn with her left hand and managed to wrench that wrist in the process. After her less than graceful decent to the ground, she walked her horse the last half-mile. Lexie didn't have the strength to loosen Blue's girth. Still, he was breathing normally and was cool when she traded him with Sam for her dog.

******

By the time Cutter arrived in the wake of the bane of his once peaceful existence, Lexie was gone again. He questioned Maria. "Did my wife tell you where she was going?"

"No, Cutter, she came in, gathered her purse and her dog, and then left. She doesn't talk to me—ever."

Cutter was aggravated that Lexie had managed to make another escape before he could fully explain about the morning ride and the disclosure of the rescued Lazy K stock. "Well, Maria, it appears Lex can hold a grudge and is unlikely to forget insults or bad behavior from anyone."

He figured that she went to town to get away from him or to have lunch there again. But when he returned to the barn to take care of his stallion, Sam asked him if his wife had been thrown or had sustained an accident with Blue.

"Not as far as I know, but she kept going when I got waylaid by Jim and Pete. Why?"

"She led him back and left him with me. I noticed she was holding her arm at a strange angle and limping. Mrs. Ross said she hadn't had any problem with the horse. Then she told me, 'I am only tired, and out of my mind for returning to this God forsaken place.' I swear, Cutter, those were her exact words. I took care of Blue, but I heard her vehicle roar out of the drive a short time later."

Cutter was concerned about Sam's description of his wife's condition, but was relieved when he checked to find she hadn't packed her laptop or any of her clothing. He hoped she was merely avoiding him and cooling off her explosive temper. He intended to tear Lubbock apart looking for her if she wasn't back by dinner.

He wished once again that he could get his hands on Sophie's grandson. Decker's blatant disregard for the consequences of his actions, were spilling over onto the Rocking R and into Cutter's rocky new marriage. He hoped that Booker came through with the legal owners of the cattle now recuperating on the eastern border of the ranch. He was worried about the legalities of removing someone else's cattle from their property, even if it was to keep them from starving to death. It could easily be construed as rustling.

******

Lexie used her maiden name when she signed in at the walk in-clinic, but her signature was barely legible even though she printed. Unable to use her right hand, she tried her less-damaged left and was amazed at how difficult it was to accomplish the small task. Fortunately, all of her identification was still in her own name. She thought about the relief she felt at using the Parker name, am I ready to call it quits after only four days?

She was mortified. The x-rays and the procedure that involved placing the cast on her right arm weren't bad, but the female doctor insisted on a complete examination when she saw the obvious finger-shaped marks on her wrists. The discovery of bruises in some intimate places caused the doctor to check her internally. Then, the doctor asked if she wanted to press charges. She was in such a hurry to shower and talk to her departing mother that she hadn't bothered to take inventory of the nagging aches and pains. Lexie was more shocked than the doctor at her condition. She'd been ouchy for days following their brief honeymoon. So like then, she chalked it up to her inexperience and their size disparity. She wondered if she should keep on going until she got to Ohio. How many times had she urged friends to get out of an abusive relationship? Was she now in one of them? Had he purposely tried to hurt her?

The pros and cons of returning to the ranch bounced around in her mind while she and Skip shared lunch at a table set outside a burger joint. She placed a call to Mel while she was waiting for the doctor to read the x-rays, but it rolled over to her friend's voice mail. Mel returned the call while she and her furry pal munched on their burgers and fries.

"Hi, Lexie! Sorry I didn't get back to you quicker. Dad and I went to the airport to pick up Booker and your mom. My phone was almost dead, so I left it on the charger. How is married life out on the open range?"

"Things aren't going well at all. Cutter is really worked up about the fire at Decker's old place. The reason he came back home so fast was that one of his hands had been arrested on suspicion of arson, and because of the potential of the fire spreading to his ranch. Mom blurted out that I had contacted Booker while he was here and the fact that we had lunch with him while she and I were in town. Cutter has been pissed because I won't tell him what is going on. He was drinking last night and we got into a huge battle of wills. I punched him and fractured my damned arm. I came to town to get it set. I called you while I was at the clinic."

"Is Cutter there with you?"

"No. Just me and Skip."

"You mean he let you drive yourself with a broken arm?"

"Not exactly. He doesn't know about it, and I don't think he really cares one way or the other anyway. The only things he cares about are exercising his marital rights and interrogating me about the goings on at the other ranch. To say the least, if I'd any idea what life here was going to be like, I would still be in Ohio."

"That doesn't sound like him, Lexie."

"Oh, he's Sir Galahad as long as things go his way."

"Has he reneged on any of his pre-nup agreements with you?"

"No. Not yet, but I have only been back here four days."

"God, Lexie, tell him what is going on. Don't mess up your chances at happiness because I made a stupid mistake in choosing a man."

"I may not have any choice in the matter for the moment. I don't think that I can make the trip home in my current condition. But you better believe that I am going to keep Skip close from now on."

******

Cutter was beginning to pace the confines of the ranch office. Where the hell is she? Maybe she already left my sorry ass and is halfway back to Ohio. His thoughts were running rampant; each time he tried to reach her by phone it rolled over to voicemail. Dinner hour was quickly approaching, and he didn't have a clue where his wife was. A minor mishap with Pete's beater truck distracted him for a couple of hours. By the time he finished helping with repairs on the old beater, her Suburban was back in its usual spot near the house parked next to his Yukon.

She wasn't in their room, but he decided to take a shower to calm his frayed nerves before he sought her out. He hadn't realized how tense he was until it flowed from his body along with a deep sigh of relief at her return. Now, if he could only wash the rest of his frustration and residual anger down the drain.

Daniel's trepidation on bearding the lion was trivial compared to the knots in his stomach. The lock on the hall door of the adjoining room her mother had recently vacated that morning was engaged. Skip sat up, alert, tracking his approach through the connecting bath. His elusive wife was sprawled across the bed with her grandmother's quilt covering her petite form. He spoke her name softly. She was deep asleep and didn't respond. He sat on the side of the bed, but was distracted by a prescription on the nightstand. "Vicodin?" No wonder she was unresponsive; an unfamiliar doctor had issued the order for the drug. He gently shook her shoulder. "Lex, come on, wake up."

She thought she heard his voice, but was having trouble leaving the peaceful void she was experiencing. Someone was shaking her and demanding she wake. When it finally penetrated her snug little cocoon that Cutter had his hands on her, she bolted upright. The protective insulation of the quilt and dreamless sleep vanished to be replaced with harsh reality.

Cutter felt like an ogre when he saw the panic in her blue eyes. She tried to scoot away from him, but was hampered not only by the quilt now around her legs but a cast from wrist to elbow on her right arm. He didn't want to upset her more so he tabled the discussion he really intended to have with her. "It is dinner time."

"I'm not hungry, Cutter."

"You didn't have breakfast. Did you eat lunch?"

"Skip and I had a burger in town."

"Ten minutes, Lex. If you aren't at the dining table, I will come back and carry you to the dining room. Do you need help getting out of that bed?"

No verbal response. She shook her head indicating she didn't need his assistance. It was obvious to him she wasn't going to make a move until he vacated the room. She used every minute of the ten he had given her before she appeared at the dinner table.

Lexie didn't know how she was going to accomplish a meal; the finger food at lunch had proved to be an ordeal. Now what was he up to? Like some kind of a Galahad he pulled out her chair and seated her at the table. Just her luck! Here she thought she had found the love of her life, but the man was either bipolar or plagued by a multiple personality disorder. She decided there was a lot to be said in favor of long engagements. She managed to take a few swallows of tea manipulating the large glass with her left hand. It was a relief when he left the table to enter the cook's sanctuary; he'd been watching her like he expected her to dump the glass in her lap, or all over the table.

The truth was Cutter had no idea how badly his wife was incapacitated, or how she had gotten that way. He had to subdue her last night in self-defense, but he was relatively sure he hadn't hurt her. Cutter found what he was looking for, and left instructions for Maria in serving the dinner.

He was back. Before regaining his seat at the table, he placed a flex straw in her glass. It looked very much like the kind of straw she'd used when she woke up in the hospital. Dinner turned out to be more of a quandary for her than the manipulating of a knife and fork essentially one-handed. As usual, Maria served Cutter first, but that was where the routine went south of the border. He cut his steak into small bite size pieces, peeled his baked potato, buttered a hard roll, and then set the plate in front of her. She thought she had his number, and now he was messing with her mind. Good manners required she acknowledge him.

"Thank you."

Jim had joined them, and looked horrified at her condition. "Sam told me he thought you were thrown this morning and got hurt. I was tossed once, and it laid me up for months. So, you got off lucky. Maybe you should ride old Blaze next time?"

It looked like poor Blue was getting the blame for her injuries. Rather than manufacturing a complete fabrication, or admitting the facts she let his comments pass. "I'll give it some thought, Jim, but I don't think I'll be riding anything for a while."

She absently gave her dog some of the huge steak, and had the pleasure of hearing Maria growl under her breath, so she threw him two more bites and glared back at her. The Vicodin was wearing off, and the returning pain was not helping her disposition. She excused herself and began to rise, only to be assisted by the considerate man she had married. However, she now knew the other dominant aggressor was in there too.

Skip followed her down the hall and by the time she was able to fill her glass at the bathroom sink Cutter was there too. She gave him a wide berth and picked up the prescription bottle, but the child-safe cap was thwarting her. He took the pill container from her grip to twist it open and shake one of the wondrous pills into her palm.

"Let's have our dessert in the office where we can have some privacy."

Lexie figured she didn't have much choice. She knew when she'd made the decision to return that afternoon an interrogation was inevitable, but she was keeping Skip with her. When she entered her former workspace she saw a fresh glass of tea complete with a straw on the modest-sized table, flanked on either side by a new upholstered armchair in a light tan fabric. She chose the seat near the glass of tea. She was beginning to feel somewhat better.

"Did Blue dump you after you left me in the dust?"

"No. He was a sweetheart. I was barely able to hold on to the reins, and only had the use of leg aids to guide him. The longer we rode the worse my arm got."

"Then, your arm was already injured?"

"Jeez, Cutter, you're really quick on the uptake."

"Why the hell didn't you tell me you were hurt?"

"I did when you first suggested the ride."

"The hell you did! You only said you weren't feeling up to it, and I thought you were trying to avoid me."

"Well…there was that, too."

"Look, Lex, I didn't mean to hurt you. I was attempting to keep you from punching my lights out."

"You didn't fracture my arm; if you had, I would be well on my way home by now, regardless of the difficulty driving in my current condition. I was off balance when I struck out at you and my arm took the brunt of it. The sprain in my left wrist resulted when I slipped dismounting and reached for the horn to steady myself."

"You are too damn stubborn. If you'd told me, we could have called Doc Callahan and had that taken care of a lot earlier."

"Right! And how were you going to explain the injuries? Blue wouldn't have been able to take the blame at that point."

"I don't have to explain anything to him, or anyone else."

That answer deflated her flicker of hope for their future. Cutter was lord of the manor, and as such was beyond reproach. She changed the subject and filled him in on the goings on regarding Decker's old place. She added the fact that the new owner of the Lazy K was a real estate and land holding company that Benson Potter owned a considerable interest in. The news that the body recovered from the ruins had not yet been identified wound up her account. She still kept the threats on her person behind closed lips.

"Are you telling me that Decker drugged Melinda and kept her imprisoned at that ranch while you were out of commission?"

"And after. Mel was so under his control that she severed our friendship and sent me packing."

"No wonder Benson is intent on revenge. His daughter was abused to the point she miscarried."

"How is what Decker did to Mel any different than what you did to me last night? He used drugs to force her to his will, and you used your superior size and weight to force me to yours."

"Lex, you're my wife and I love you. It's not the same at all."

"Don't you think David told Mel repeatedly that he loved her, and proposed to boot? He really did his research and had her trust fund as well as her family money in his crosshairs. But let's get back to you and me. Because we have a marriage license, you have the right to abuse me any time the urge strikes you. Have I got the difference straight?"

"It is no excuse, but I lost my temper after you knocked the wind out of me so easily. Lex, I don't recall more than a token resistance from you."

"If you hadn't tossed me around like a damn football or a no-account rag doll, I wouldn't have tried to eliminate your drunken ass. Because you know how to manipulate a woman's body doesn't give you the right to use it against me. Should you ever go for a replay of last night's assault Cutter, it will be the end. If one of us isn't pushing up daisies, Mr. Potter will be serving you with divorce papers."

Cutter filed away her objection to his behavior the night before along with the wealth of new information she'd supplied him about recent events at the Lazy K. The revelation that Benson Potter was in effect the new owner relieved his anxiety about the rescued cattle. By the time he returned from ferrying their empty glasses and pie plates, she was sound asleep in the armchair. She didn't wake or make a sound as he scooped her up or when he deposited her back on the bed where he had found her earlier. Removing her shoes, he covered her with the precious quilt that she'd brought from Ohio; it obviously brought her comfort. He potted Skip and returned him to take up his post at the foot of her bed.

It had always been his experience that women catered to him and wanted to please him, but he'd always had the feeling they were more interested in his bank account than him as a man. He had a lot of empathy for Melinda Potter. His wife, however, had no interest in his wealth, but she didn't mind taking a pot shot at him for bad behavior. If he could make amends and keep her from packing up and heading back to Yankee-land, he had a feeling their married life was going to be anything but dull.

Cutter worked late and went to bed alone. He didn't want to trust himself to move her into his bed. He wasn't old enough to sleep close to her without wanting more; he wasn't sure he ever would be that old. He was determined not to make the mistakes that Grandpa Cutter accused Cutter's dad of making with his own mother, but he was off to a miserable start.

He woke to the sound of shattering glass along with a familiar Yankee string of curse words coming from the bath. He barreled through the door on his side in time to hear her order Skip to stay. Then she turned to him and, in the same tone she'd used with her dog, she warned him to stop. She gave his naked body a worried glance.

"There is glass everywhere; you'll cut your feet."

He pulled on his Wranglers and boots, not bothering with the whole underwear issue, and for the second night in succession, retrieved the broom and dustpan after commanding her to stay put. She was worried about everyone else, but was standing in the middle of the glass shards barefoot. Cutter picked her up and deposited her into the bedroom next to Skip.

Lexie scrounged up her shoes while he cleaned up her mess. When he took the swept-up glass to dispose of it, she seized the opportunity to enter his room and secure one of her oversized tees to sleep in instead of her clothing. He came back before she could exit.

"What are you doing, Lex?"

"Getting something other than my clothes to sleep in." He was standing in his room's open door bare-chested, his jeans only partially buttoned up and looking too male and predatory for her comfort. She began to retreat toward the bathroom as he moved in her direction. He stopped at the closet to remove a blue plaid shirt. He took her tee from her hand and replaced it with the snap front shirt.

"You will find this easier to get into. Did you take your medication?"

"No. I dropped the glass trying to fill it. Don't you have any non-breakable glasses in this place of super hard floors?"

"I guess we'll have to purchase some."

He had the gall to grin at her disgusted epitaphs before he turned and walked down the hall. She beat a hasty retreat to the other bedroom and was struggling to unhook her bra when he returned. He set a plastic bottle of water on the nightstand, and then moved behind her to unhook her before continuing on to his room, closing the bathroom door on his way through. Lexie finished undressing and struggled into the hauntingly familiar blue plaid. He had loosened the cap on the water, so it was not difficult for her to remove it to down the pain reliever. Less than twenty minutes later, she was in a restful, deep sleep.

Cutter didn't see much point in returning to bed for less than two hours. Getting a head start on his day might allow him to take his wife to lunch, and shop for some non-breakable glasses and cups.

******

Lexie got a smaller cast on her damaged right arm the end of October, and only required an ace bandage on her left wrist for support during the day. She resumed her bookkeeping duties as well as her riding. Blue was her mount when he was available, but on the days Cutter used him for ranch work, she rode old Blaze. She confined her equestrian exercise to the indoor arena or the back pen where they started the colts. Skip was still with her. The Williams boys had come and gone twice, but she was reluctant to let Skip go. He was her company, her only friend—or so she believed—and he was unfailingly loyal. He wouldn't understand if she sent him away, and Skip seemed to be settling in better than she was. He was even becoming attached to Cutter. She still slept in the other bedroom, but was only taking the medication at night, or if she overdid things and her right arm was giving her fits. The pain reliever made her nauseous.

November brought much-needed rain and bouts of cool weather. Lexie made a trip to Lubbock mid-month to get her cast removed, and received instructions not to take any more Vicodin. The doctor was also concerned about her habit of skipping meals. She was given vitamins and a prescription to combat her frequent and hasty trips to the bathroom. It had been difficult to get away for this appointment without Cutter. Ever vigilant, he didn't think she should make the long trip alone. Lexie headed back to the ranch rather than taking time to shop and have to listen to another lecture. Thank God she and Skip had eaten lunch in Lubbock. The smell of the enchiladas and refried beans that Maria had prepared for lunch sent her touchy stomach rolling. She made an iced tea, filled Skip's water dish, and retired to the office to work on the books. It had bothered her at first that her faithful dog couldn't have the run of the house the way he had at home, but he didn't seem to mind.

A few days later, she was on her way back from a late morning workout with Blue when she caught the distinct scent of sauerkraut as it wafted past her. She hadn't run across that aroma since leaving Ohio; it would have been an understatement to say the smell made her homesick. Intrigued, she wandered over to the cookhouse and introduced herself to Ollie, the new cook for the crew. He served her a plate of heaven. She hadn't had bratwurst since she and Mel used to visit the German Village in Columbus. Several times that week she shared lunch with the hands. Of course, word got back to her husband.

Cutter was getting a lot of razzing about his wife hanging out with the cowhands. He hadn't thought much about her absence from the noon meal; she often worked through lunch. He decided to confront her about the inappropriate behavior. It galled him that she would spend time with the men at the cookhouse rather than have lunch with him. As he'd suspected, she was working on the computer. He sat in his old leather chair and waited for her to acknowledge him.

Lexie finished the entries she was working on and hit save before she raised questioning eyes to her husband. It was obvious from his clenched jaw and cool gray eyes that he had a bone to pick with her. "Okay, now what did I do to piss you off?"

"It has come to my attention that you have been having your lunch at the cookhouse with the ranch hands."

"So?"

"So, it's not appropriate for you to be fraternizing with the hired help. You can have lunch here with your husband, like a respectable wife."

"Are you telling me I am not supposed to associate with anyone on this ranch but you?"

"I don't think you should be spending time there with other men."

"Fine, every other day I will go to Lubbock for lunch, or you can get me a microwave and small fridge for the office."

"Lex, you're being unreasonable. There is plenty of food in the kitchen, and Maria is an excellent cook."

"The mere smell of that Tex-Mex slop is beginning to turn my stomach."

"You're acting like a child in the throes of a temper tantrum. I think it is about time you started acting like a grown-up married woman. That includes sharing my bed now that you are no longer in constant pain."

He waited for an argument that never came. She just turned extremely pale at his comment. She got up from behind the desk and walked out of the room followed by her dog. Cutter followed in her wake after he got his temper under control. He found her emptying her dresser to throw the contents on the bed. When she hauled out her luggage, he intervened, taking it from her grasp. "What the hell are you doing?"

"Going home."

"This is your home now. Are you planning on running back to Mommy every time we have a disagreement?"

She merely glared at him, took off her rings, and threw them at him. He left the room to keep from strangling her, and then he made a call to Jim. "You need to handle things. I will be unavailable for the remainder of the day." "There is no way in hell she is going to pack up and leave." He grumbled to himself after disconnecting his cell as he wandered back down the hall.

Lexie started ferrying her packed luggage down the hall, only to be thwarted by her bully of a husband. Cutter literally yanked the traveling cases from her grip. Her wrists weren't back to a hundred percent, but she doubted it would have made much difference. She took a swing at him. He was prepared this time, and avoided her intended blow. She was scooped up like a sack of grain and thrown across his shoulder; then he smacked her on the posterior to add to the insult, and carted her back down the hall. Once again, he threw her on his bed, warning her not to move. He removed Skip, she assumed to the office. Feeling ill, she hurried to the bathroom to lose the meager contents of her stomach and was seized with a bout of dry heaves. She rinsed out her mouth and went into the room she'd been occupying since she fractured her arm. That is where he found her. He was angry that she'd, in his view, defied his order to stay put.

Cutter was at the end of his rope. He'd given her plenty of time to heal and come around. It appeared to him that she was settling in, but now she was ready to chuck their marriage and return to Ohio. If she thought she could avoid him by retreating to this room, he was about to debunk her of that notion. He got in the smaller bed and pulled her beneath him.

Lexie was terrified of a repeat assault like the last time he forced her onto a bed and pinned her beneath his much larger body. She began to cry hysterically. "Get off me!"

Anger he could handle, but her uncontrolled weeping and the panic in her eyes undid him. However, he was reluctant to let her up; he knew she was still intent on packing up and heading north. "Lex, calm down so we can hash this out."

"If you rape me again, I will file a police report this time. You may not care about me, but you could damage the baby."

The shot he took in the abdomen wasn't nearly as painful as his wife accusing him of rape. Admittedly things had gotten out of hand the night she was injured, but… "What?"

"You heard me. I will fill out a police report."

"No—you aggravating woman, the part about the baby."

"I am not telling you anything else until you get off of me and let me up so I can get the pill I came in here for."

Cutter let her up and watched her take a pill from a bottle kept in the small drawer of the nightstand. When she went to the sink for a glass of water he looked over the label. "When were you going to tell me that you were pregnant, Lex?"

He had thought the evening before his drunken botch job of their promising relationship that she was likely to have conceived. That speculative moment had slipped from his mind with all the recent turmoil.

"I hadn't made up my mind until your obvious disapproval of me came to light a short while ago. At that point, I decided not to tell you and return home."

"Lex, at the risk of sounding like a broken record, this is your home."

"No, Cutter, this is your home, and it is more Maria's home than mine. I'm a virtual prisoner in this house, confined to spending my time in here or in the office to keep from causing another confrontation or uproar in your home. Now you tell me I can't associate with the only humans within fifty miles because they happen to be male. I am going home where I can follow doctor's orders by eating three meals a day of regular food without someone making a big deal of where and what I eat. For your information, most of my friends have always been male. Mel is one of the few exceptions. You seem to be the only one of your gender that I can't get along with, which doesn't paint a bright future for us."

He had to admit that he was out working the better part of most days, and had little knowledge of what it was like to be confined. He agreed to take her to lunch and shop for the microwave and the fridge if she would give it a shot until the first of the year.

Lexie released her dog from his confinement on the way out the door, while Cutter informed Maria they would be having lunch in Lubbock. She thought that news probably went over like a lead balloon. Cutter glanced at Skip in the backseat and his eyebrows came very close to being a unibrow, but he didn't make an issue of the dog accompanying them.

******

They had completed the purchases of the appliances for the office along with a couple of microwavable bowls and utensils. Cutter had intended to take her to one of the better restaurants in town, but she only wanted a burger and fries. So they sat at an outdoor table with their lunch. Skip was busy on his plain burger when he suddenly jumped up, alert to something neither one of them could see or hear. An old blue pickup rounded the corner of the nearby intersection, slowed up, and then the driver threw a burlap bag out the passenger side window before picking up speed and roaring away. Skip took off at a dead run out into the busy road with two much slower humans in hot pursuit. Cutter's longer legs got to her dog as he was dragging the bag from the street. He relieved Skip of the burden.

Lexie was about to ask what was in the old feedbag when the cry of little puppies came from inside it. "Oh, my God! How could anyone do something like that?"

Cutter didn't say anything, and refused to let her look in the bag until they arrived at the nearest vet's office. The vet carefully took the puppies one by one from their burlap prison. Out of seven tiny canines only four were still alive, and the vet didn't hold out much hope for the smallest pup.

Rose Jenkins D.V.M. wanted to keep the pups for a couple of days for observation. Lexie said she would be back in two days to pick up the survivors.

"They're going to need a lot of care for a while, Mrs. Ross, it doesn't look like they are quite old enough to be weaned."

Cutter relented when she said she wanted the puppies. He figured it would give her something to focus on other than thoughts of how to escape from him. He probably would not have been so quick to agree to the adoption of the remaining four puppies if he'd had a clue as to the resulting turmoil.

CHAPTER 8

Thanksgiving came and went. Lexie was relieved to find a traditional turkey for dinner on the usually poultry-free cook's menu, but the bird was stuffed with some rice concoction instead of the traditional bread stuffing she was accustomed to. But Ollie came through with a care package of stuffing and gravy. When he had found out she wasn't permitted to eat at the cookhouse any longer he brought her little care packages several times a week. With his help, her new fridge, and microwave she was able to eat more often.

The puppies were also on their way to better nutrition. They were wolfing down solid food now, and beginning to climb out of their little nest in the tall cardboard box that she and Cutter had rigged up for them. Lexie figured that on the next trip to town she needed to get a playpen to confine the rambunctious little devils. They were really cute; Doc Rose thought they looked like a Hound-Rottweiler mix. Two were black and tan with the typical markings of a Rottweiler, but all had the look of a hound. One male sported the coat as well as the look of a blue tick, and the tiny female was black with a white patch on her chest, and four white paws. Ollie had spoken up for the blue tick, and Sam wanted the black and tan male. It was no surprise to Lexie that in this male dominated society the two females were unspoken for.

Her planned trip to town was put on hold. Five days after Thanksgiving, they were hit with a winter storm. Sleet and snow pummeled them for the better part of a day and a half. Then it got warm again and the white blanket turned to mud.

The first day of the storm, Cutter stayed close and spent more time in the house. The tiny, black puppy took a fancy to him. She followed him whenever he entered the confines of the office and kept jumping up on his pant leg until he picked her up to pay attention to her.

Skip took on the duty of shepherding the little ones that he had pulled from the road. They were beginning to scamper around and were prone to darting out the door when people entered or left the office. The female black and tan pup was very quick and she wanted to explore the great beyond. Her urge to break out into the larger world almost cost her life.

Lexie and Skip had returned from a short morning run with Blue. As luck would have it, they came across Cutter on his way back from the eastern boundary where the Lazy K herd was kept. The small herd now numbered twenty-eight. He was worried that the weakened cattle may not have fared well under the ice storm. He was making her crazy. Ever since she had blurted out that she was in a family way he didn't want her riding alone, driving alone, or lifting anything heavier than one of the puppies. Lord have mercy, she prayed. I'm not even a full three months yet. Cutter took her horse to remove the tack, instead of letting her do it, and put him away in addition to his own. It wasn't worth the inevitable argument. Lexie sighed in exasperation and headed for the house.

"Skip, *komm bitte*, and let's get cleaned up. We'll take the puppies outdoors for a while, after lunch."

Lexie freshened up and was on her way back up the long hall toward the kitchen when she heard a crash followed by a string of curses in a distinctly Spanish dialect. She picked up her pace to check out the ruckus the cook was making. A small black and tan form appeared from the dining room to investigate, about the same time she and Skip entered from the hall. Maria was busy sweeping up what looked like a shattered baking dish.

Lexie was about to ask if she could help—at home it would have been a no-brainer; she would have merely pitched in—when Maria let out an earsplitting screech before taking the broom and smacking the puppy.

Lexie yelled "NO!" too late. The small canine yelped like it was mortally wounded, and fell on its side. Skip was showing all the signs of having the cook for lunch. "Easy, Skip. I got it." She turned around and took a swing at Maria, then scooped up the still breathing puppy and ran down the hall for her handbag and keys. On her way out the front door, she closed Skip in the office ordering him, in her grandmother's language, *"Schütz die Welpen!"* She knew the other pups would come to no harm with Skip ordered to guard them, and she hurried out the door with the injured puppy.

Cutter had just finished with the horses and was headed to the house for lunch. Jim and Sam were accompanying him when his wife came barreling through the door carrying one of the puppies. She didn't bother to acknowledge any of them. In a flash she was into her Suburban. It was obvious she was distraught and in no condition to drive. She reluctantly surrendered her keys to him along with the driving duties.

"Hurry, Cutter. I think she's dying!"

"What happened Lex?"

"I don't know how she got out, but Maria tried to kill her with a broom."

She wasn't in any condition to argue with him when he said he doubted that Maria had tried to kill the pup. Her inability to staunch the tears, and her rising nausea made it impossible to take him to task for once again coming to Maria's defense.

"Stop! Cutter, pull over!"

He replied to the urgency in her voice. The vehicle had barely stopped when she flung the door open, handed him the puppy, and went to the side of the road to lose what was left of her breakfast.

The animal hospital was busy that afternoon, but they rushed the pup to one of the emergency rooms. Lex explained how the injuries occurred to the vet assistant, who immediately interrupted Doc Rose for an evaluation. X-rays were ordered.

Lexie and Cutter were excused to the waiting room for eternity. In real time it was only short of two hours. When they saw the pup again, she had a cast on her right front leg, and a size appropriate needle taped to her other leg that was attached to an IV.

Leaving her there was one of the toughest things Lexie'd ever had to do. The x-rays hadn't shown any additional broken bones, and the ultrasounds hadn't detected internal damage. The pup was in shock, and there was always the possibility of damage to her brain. The blow had driven her head and body onto the hard surface of the kitchen floor, resulting in a swelling of her brain. She didn't have a name yet, so Lexie shared hers; little Alex would be under observation for several days.

Cutter insisted on lunch before returning to the ranch. That was fine with her. She wasn't in a big hurry to get arrested for assault. If Maria was still there when she got back she was going to mop the floor with the hateful woman. Lexie excused herself, once their order was placed, to make use of the ladies' room to wash her face and hands, and then she downed one of the pills to prevent another bout queasiness that would result in losing her yet-to-be-eaten lunch.

When she returned to the table, the chicken dumpling soup had arrived. Cutter folded his cell phone and returned it to the frayed worn leather carrier on his belt. Lexie knew she was going to be given another lecture about her inappropriate behavior by the way he was looking at her and frowning. Fortunately, he waited until they finished lunch and were on their way back to the ranch.

"I checked with Jim before lunch; Dr. Callahan was with Maria. She told him that you punched her in the face when he asked how she broke her nose."

Lexie didn't answer him, but she felt immense satisfaction at the news.

"Lex, did you punch her in the face?"

"You're damn right I did, and if I get my hands on her, I am going to break a lot more than her nose."

"Maria was so upset about the accident, Joe gave her a sedative to calm her down."

"Accident my ass! I was there, Cutter, she intended to kill that pup. She wasn't merely shooing it out of the kitchen."

"It was a mistake, Lex. She thought it was a rat."

"Oh, give me a break, Cutter. When have you ever seen a rat in the house?"

"It happens. It's usually after a flash flood, or following a bad winter storm."

"Well, that's just fine, Cutter. You can continue to make excuses for her, but should you ever take my side that would really be monumental."

"Do you expect me to take your side even when you're wrong?"

"God forbid. You have a choice to make; it's her or me. I refuse to live like this or subject our child to that hateful person."

She didn't speak to him again the rest of the way home. As soon as he parked, she quickly entered the house to check on the other puppies. Maria was not in the house; he was grateful for that small reprieve. He drove over to the Rodriguez bungalow to have a talk with Jim and his wife.

Lexie cleaned up behind the puppies, then took them and Skip out to play in what she was reluctant to call a yard. They were pretty good at using the puppy pads she had put down for them, but they occasionally missed the mark. It was time to make more of an effort to housebreak them. She returned the puppies to the office and secured the door. She still couldn't figure out how little Alex had gotten out.

Maria hadn't returned and it was almost dinnertime. Lexie stiffened her spine and entered the self-imposed restricted domain of the cook. She didn't see anything that looked like it was set side for dinner. She went into the small fridge in the office, looking for salad items and her favorite dressing. The mystery of the puppy's escape became apparent; tucked on one of the two shelves was a large container of veal paprika. Skip herded the three remaining pups out of the way so that she could get through the door. She placed her haul on the kitchen table before she returned to retrieve her canine helper, and close the puppies in again.

"Okay, Skip, I think we can reheat the veal that Ollie left for us, add a salad and the rolls I found in the bread box for a decent dinner for the three of us. I only hope he doesn't drag anyone else home with him today, if he even shows up. I have a hunch you and I will be hitting the road fairly soon."

Cutter showed up in time for dinner, but even his sparse one or two word commentaries were conspicuously absent. And so it went over the next few days, they barely spoke. He was definitely not pleased with the absence of his precious Maria.

Lexie was not inclined to ask her husband about Maria's condition and suffer his disapproval again, so she asked Sam.

"Jim says she looks like a raccoon with a broken snout. But it's her depression that really concerns him."

"I didn't think I hit her hard enough to do all that damage."

"She was sprawled on the floor in the middle of some broken glass and uncooked enchiladas, bawling like a baby about killing another dog. Her nose was bleeding unnoticed down the front of her onto the floor. It took the two of us to move her from the floor to a chair. I got some ice for her nose while Jim called Doc Joe."

Lexie had to admit she hadn't given Maria a second thought; her focus had been entirely on the injured puppy. It broke her heart that after all the survivors of the brutally abandoned litter had been through one of them could come to harm in what should have been the safe confines of the house.

The following morning, once Cutter was off on the far reaches of the ranch, she went to check on little Alex. The pup was off the IV and trying to wobble around on her cast. She was eating and drinking, but the vet and her assistant said she was standoffish and unsocial. However, she came right up to Lexie, wagging her tail and giving a joyful little bark. Lexie spent some time with her, and the vet was impressed with the pup's response.

Lexie went shopping while she was in town. She purchased four doggy beds, two blue collars, two red collars and a dog carrier for the car. The carrier would come in handy for the puppies' vet checkup in two days when she picked up Alex.

She got back before Cutter, successfully avoiding another confrontation about her blatant disregard for his wishes on a multitude of fronts. She busied herself frying the chicken she had picked up at the grocer's in town, and preparing the rest of the dinner.

Not one word about her skills or lack of as a cook. What he wanted to know was where was she ate lunch, and where she got the chicken. Then she had to listen to him scold her like she was a child or a simpleton unable to manage menial tasks like going to town to check on the injured puppy, or going to the grocery.

"Cutter, I am going to town again the day after tomorrow. I have an appointment to take the puppies for a checkup and their shots. I will also be bringing Alex back. At that time, I will hand the boys over to their new owners. Skip, the two little girl puppies, and I will be out of here. You can move Maria back in as soon as we are gone. You will be much happier when things are back to the status quo, and your inappropriate witch of a wife is out of your life."

He downed the remainder of his coffee and set the mug down hard enough to break it and dent the oak dining table. He turned at the mudroom door after adjusting his black Stetson, "You can leave Bib here; she's my dog." He snatched his jacket off the peg, grabbed a pair of work gloves from the shelf, and was gone.

Bib? She wasn't aware he'd named the little black and white puppy that liked him so much. She sure hoped the little runt, that had beat unbelievable odds, fared better with him than she was able to. Lexie wondered whether it was their very different upbringing, their social economic status being diametrically opposed, or the eight years separating them that kept them from gaining any unity.

Cutter didn't even come home that night, or the following night. He didn't show up for breakfast the morning of the puppies' checkup. Lexie placed the three pups in the new carrier and made the trip out the side kitchen entrance where she had last seen her husband. There, waiting to assist her with loading the dog carrier was Pete. It appeared that he had been assigned to ride shotgun for the day. She returned to the house for Skip, his water bowl, another one for the pups, and a half-gallon jug of water.

Skip occupied the back seat and kept an eye on the little ones confined in the dog crate sitting in the cargo area. A good hour passed before Lexie's curiosity got the better of her. "Pete, how did you get the dubious honor of accompanying me today?"

"Don't really know, ma'am. Ever since I come to work fir Cutter, I been assistin' Sam with the hosses. Mostly, they give me the soft jobs. But yesterday, Sam says Cutter has a dangerous assignment fir me. He tells me I got to stick with you today, no matter how ornery you get, or how much you object. He offered me hazard pay."

"Cutter offered you hazard pay just to ride to town with me?"

"Yes ma'am, he surely did!"

Lexie broke into a fit of laughter. Once she got herself under control, she asked, "Do you know where he is, Pete?"

"Sam said somphen' bout' a quarter year trip to Dallas."

Pete didn't know much more than she did, but at least she knew where he was. She wondered if the family attorneys he had once mentioned once were based in Dallas. Maybe he figured he would beat her to the punch on the divorce issue.

******

Cutter was having a hard time keeping his head in the board meeting. He had taken the place of his maternal grandfather, at the elder's request, after Ben Cutter had a stroke. Ben had only lived a little more than a year after that, and he was the last link to Cutter's long dead mother. In addition to the trust funds left to him and his brother when they were each born, his grandfather had left Cutter with the bulk of his wealth, as well as his seat on the board of Cutter Inc. Nothing much got past him; Grandpa Ben had groomed him well. The years he spent working with him while he attended A&M paid off with unexpected dividends. Diversification kept the company in the black when a lot of their original competition sank in the struggling economy and the unprecedented drought. Ben's savvy grandson applied the same philosophy to his personal holdings. Rarely did he lose his temper. Well, not until a little blonde with blue eyes slid off the road and into his life earlier in the year.

He wasn't up to the usual schmoozing. He retired to the company-owned penthouse suite and ordered in. It worried him that Lexie was alone in the house, if she was even still there. He didn't remember his mother being so all-fired independent and disagreeable, but then he was only a child. His mother had loved him and his brother Ben; he could remember the love, but his recollection of her face and physical form had faded with time. It was his grandfather's old photos of his mother as a girl that had brought back some warmer moments of his childhood.

Cutter had buried himself in his studies, and then the demands of the business as well as the day-to-day operation of the ranch, until the lack of love in his life became the norm. It was hard for him to admit, even to himself, that the past loss of loved ones affected the way he dealt with his wife. She meant more to him than he was willing to let her know. She could already tie him in knots and cause him to lose his objectivity as well as his temper.

He would give her a call after dinner. Maybe he could determine her whereabouts and her current frame of mind. She had almost three days to cool off. He sure hoped she had and perhaps she missed him as much as he was missing her. He missed the laughter, the arguments, and even the frustration she caused him, but mostly he missed holding her close to him through the night.

*****

Lexie decided to confront the lioness in her den on the morning of the third day of Cutter's absence. She had been trying to get a handle on Maria since she discovered that Cutter had given her two weeks' severance pay—in effect firing his longtime cook and housekeeper. Lexie's assessment of a vindictive backstabber didn't match Cutter's view of Maria, or even come close. The ranch hands including Maria's husband Jim didn't shed any light either. In general, she found the male population of the Rocking R pretty clueless.

Lexie took Skip and Alex along for moral support. Maria's reaction to her chosen companions would give her a clue as to how to proceed. She was learning more about the people and the workings of the ranch since Cutter's abrupt departure. She was somewhat familiar with Sam and the horse operation. Thanks to the few lunches she'd shared at the cookhouse, she had a working knowledge of Cutter's job as well a glimpse at the life of a cowhand. She could now match up more faces to the entry names on the ranch payroll.

A half-mile from the ranch house, she was still reluctant to call home, stood a cluster of a half dozen small bungalows. Lexie located the one marked number five and pulled into the gravel drive. She scooped Alex off the front seat and let Skip out of the back. Her knock on the door was a lot more timid than her usual aggressive style. She was about ready to give up the quest when Maria opened the door. Lexie was shocked by how bad the woman still looked; her nose was splinted and both eyes were now multicolored as opposed to the black, raccoon-like mask that Maria's husband had described.

"Hello, Maria. May we come in?"

She opened the door to allow the unexpected trio to enter her home. Maria already had her tree up and decorated. Green garland was draped around the house with small silver bells hanging from it at approximately six-inch intervals. She offered Lexie tea and snickerdoodles.

"I am sorry, Mrs. Ross, but I do not have any lemon."

"Plain is tea fine, Maria. Your home is lovely and very festive."

"Thank you, but it must seem small and pathetic to you. Several of these small homes could fit inside the big house."

"Truthfully, I grew up in a home not much bigger than yours, but where I come from everyone has a basement. It affords you more living space, or room to accumulate more junk that no one ever uses."

Maria handed Skip a cookie, much to Lexie's surprise. He looked at his mistress for direction, drooling the whole time.

"It's okay, Skip."

"He is very well trained to wait for your permission. Can the puppy have some?"

"Only a small piece. She hasn't been eating solid food very long and she is still on medication."

Lexie set Alex on the floor next to Skip. She had an easier time on the small braided carpet beneath the table than she did on the hard flooring in what Maria called the big house. Little Alex mouthed the small morsel, decided it was yummy, and made quick work of it. Maria laughed at her hopeful expression.

The dogs settled down, and Skip sprawled out on the floor, resting his head on the blue and green braided oval where Alex snuggled up next to him.

Lexie sipped her warm tea, and then got to the point of her visit. "Maria, I came here today to apologize for breaking your nose. It is no excuse, but I was upset about the injury to Alex and lost my temper."

"I did not mean to hurt the puppy. She was just a small shadow scampering across the floor and I thought it was a rat when I swatted at it. I swear to you that I would never deliberately hit a dog."

Lexie believed her. Maria was wiping at the copious tears streaming down her face; she left the table to snatch a couple of tissues from the blue Formica counter behind her. While Maria pulled herself together and carefully blew her ouchy nose, Lexie scanned the kitchen. She was looking for some insight into her adversary. The light blue vinyl floor tiles were splattered with shades of gray and white, giving it a marbled look. The color scheme was carried through to a robin's egg blue paint that contrasted nicely with the white cabinets. The same shade of blue wall tile filled the space between the upper cupboards and the blue counter. Sheer café-style curtains dressed the window next to the glass-topped table with baked white enamel supports and legs. The short ladder-back chair she occupied was obviously made for the table, but the blue seat cover looked homemade, as did the rug the dogs were snoozing on.

Maria's kitchen was very modern, right up to the lighted white ceiling fan. It contrasted with the living area where she had entered. There, a large area rug in shades of tan and brown sported what looked like an oriental pattern. The lower walls were paneled with an oak finish topped by a one-inch chair rail that matched the bookcase on the wall opposite where the Christmas tree stood. An armchair, recliner, and small sofa were all tan-hued leather. The end tables, coffee tables, and the small writing desk with a matching tall ladder-backed chair all looked like well-kept antiques, the color of aged oak. Stationed opposite the door she and the dogs had recently entered was a black iron wood burner on a raised brick platform. It was about half the size of the one in Cutter's kitchen, but like it in addition to providing heat it had burners on the top to allow for cooking in a power outage. What she could see of the house was immaculate and beautifully decorated. Maria obviously took a lot of pride in making a home for her husband and herself.

Maria returned to the table to pour more tea from the small white ceramic teapot, and picked up her apology.

"Maria, I believe you. It seems not a soul on this ranch, other than myself, think you capable of such malice, including my husband. Since I had been on the receiving end of your malevolence, you may be able to understand my viewpoint."

"Jim said the reason Cutter fired me was because you told him it was you or me."

"That's true, I was angry. I was tired of trying to stay out of your way, and felt like an outsider in the house, and the incident with Alex caused me to snap. That aside, if you can keep your hatred of me under control, I would like you to come back to work."

"You want me to come back to work?" Maria was astonished.

"Yes, but there are some conditions. Your kitchen duties are confined to five days, and I will cook on your days off. If I have an uncontrollable urge to bake at night, I will use the kitchen. Since the fact that I do my laundry in Lubbock is a big issue with my husband, I will use the washer and dryer when you are not there. Hopefully, this will lighten the guilt Cutter seems to be suffering since he terminated your long-time service."

"Thank you. I would like to return to work for you and Cutter. I do not hate you, Mrs. Ross."

"You could have fooled me, Maria."

She had the grace to look embarrassed. "When do you want me to start, Mrs. Ross?"

Lexie ignored the reference to her as Mrs. Ross when Maria called Cutter by his first name, like an old friend. Since she had in effect rehired her nemesis, the employer-employee boundary might serve them better.

"You can resume your duties whenever you feel up to it, and your pay will remain the same since it's my choice that you limit your days. If you feel well enough to come over later this afternoon or tomorrow to show me where the Christmas decorations are stored, I would appreciate it."

Maria showed up later that afternoon to help her find and sort through the Christmas stash. Having her job back loosened Maria's tongue considerably, and Lexie found some of the missing pieces to the puzzle of her husband's background.

CHAPTER 9

LEXIE had a bowl of soup for dinner while she admired their handiwork. A lot had been accomplished during the afternoon, including the decorating of the large artificial tree in the front corner of the dining room. It seemed that Cutter had banned the use of real trees on the Rocking R until the drought ended. Disposing of the tinder-dry pines posed a potential fire hazard. Though it had rained and even snowed most recently, the welcome moisture was a long way from ending the drought.

She took the dogs out for a while, and checked on the progress of the dog pen she had requisitioned. Pete, with the occasional help of a younger man, had leveled and formed a spot for the cyclone fence dog enclosure she'd purchased when she had picked up the doggie beds. She'd chosen a spot toward the back of the house well past the mudroom entrance and behind the vehicle parking area. The concrete pad looked dry enough for the construction of the pen to begin within the next day or two.

It had been a long, stressful day, and she found herself nodding off over the computer entries. She backed up her work, potted the dogs once more, moved their little beds from the office to the back bedroom, closed them in, showered, and then crawled under Grandma's quilt.

******

Cutter was beat. It was well past midnight when he entered the dark house. Upon reaching the bedroom, he hesitated to turn on the light until he realized his wife was not in their shared bed. Her Suburban was still in its usual spot making him assume she was again in the adjoining room.

That was where he found her when he finished showering. Skip lifted his head, gave him a once over, and returned to his doggie dreams. The little dog with the cast hanging over her red plaid dog bed gave him a bit more scrutiny, and Bib was hopping up and down in front of him like a little windup toy. He picked her up, scratched her ears and tummy, and then deposited her back into her cozy green-and-blue sleeping quarters.

He continued over to his sleeping wife, guided by the diffused light from the attached bath. As soon as he sat on the bed, she opened her eyes and smiled at him. He kissed her with all the passion he had bottled up. When he broke off to let them both come up for air, she chose to get in a little dig at him.

"Hi stranger, where have you been all my life? It's only fair to warn you that I'm married to a man who doesn't allow me to even talk to other men, let alone kiss one like that."

He didn't say a word, but scooped her up to carry her back to their bed. He'd closed the door as they exited effectively confined the canine menagerie. He placed her on the bed and resumed where they had left off. Several hours later, he dozed off with his wife sprawled across his chest sound asleep.

Loud yelping and scraping noises woke them. Lexie groaned, yawned, and rolled over to her back. "The puppies have to go out."

He kissed her forehead. "Go back to sleep. I'll take care of them."

Lexie didn't think that her husband returned to bed after potting the dogs. He was probably out working already.

She had a breakfast of fruit, a western omelet, and blueberry muffins ready when he returned slightly past eight. He wolfed down his breakfast without comment, but frowned at the contents of his coffee mug. He didn't complain, but her efforts to brew it obviously didn't come up to his standards. She would have to ask Maria how she made it. Tea was their meal beverage of choice at home and she didn't have much experience at making coffee. Mom usually did that when she wanted a cup, or when they had coffee drinking company. Lexie merely followed the directions on the can.

"What is going on with the concrete pad out back, Lex?"

"I bought a large dog pen for the puppies, and thought it would be easier to keep it clean with a cement pad beneath it."

"You did that yourself?"

He already knew better, and was messing with her. "I asked Sam to lend me Pete for the project, since he was feeling guilty about the hazard pay thing."

"Don't you think you should have consulted me about a project like this?"

"Are you trying to pick a fight with me this morning?"

He didn't answer her. He growled deep in his throat, and snatched up a couple of muffins as he exited through the mudroom. Well, he might not like her coffee, but he sure did scarf down the muffins.

Maria showed up shortly after Cutter left, ready to go back to work. Coffee was the first topic. Lexie couldn't believe that brewing to Cutter's liking required two additional heaping scoops to the directions on the can. Maria began lunch preparations before turning her attention to the housekeeping chores.

Lexie took the morning to resume the bookkeeping task that she had abandoned the previous evening.

Cutter entered through the mudroom, shucking off his jacket, gloves, and boots; he washed and then entered the kitchen. There, going about her duties, was Maria. He thought he had made it clear that she was no longer employed as his cook and housekeeper. "Maria, what are you doing here? I know you understood that I terminated your employment."

"I know Cutter, but Mrs. Ross came to see me yesterday, and hired me back."

"She did?"

"Yes, and I am only allowed to cook five days a week, but I still get the same pay."

He sat down at the kitchen table with a mug of strong coffee, and contemplated the turn of events. It appeared that when he was absent, Lexie picked up the reins and did things her way. He was glad that Maria was back, but he wisely decided to keep out of whatever agreement they had reached. Maybe peace on earth would begin in his kitchen.

Cutter had eaten his lunch and gone back to work by the time Lexie got caught up on the books. Maria had made chili for lunch. She was busy cleaning somewhere down the hall, so Lexie gathered the ingredients for a salad, topped it off with a ladle of chili, and added a few taco chips. She was only halfway into her salad when she heard the sounds of a large truck. She ignored it, thinking it was a hay or grain delivery. A loud pounding on the side door sent Skip flying across the kitchen through the mudroom to display his razor sharp teeth. She put her fork down to see who was at the door. The deliveryman had backed down the steps; he was obviously concerned the large dog would crash the barrier between them.

Lexie put her dog at ease by ordering him to sit, but he kept his eyes on the stranger who was now talking to his mistress.

"I have a delivery for Ross at the Rocking R."

"What kind of delivery?"

"Fifty turkeys."

She didn't know anything about the delivery of turkeys. She hollered for Maria.

"Do you know anything about the delivery of fifty turkeys?"

It turned out that Maria did know about the turkey order, and thank God, they weren't the live birds, but frozen holiday gifts for the employees. Annually, the Rocking R supplied turkeys to the married hands and their families. A good number of the frozen gobblers would end up in the cookhouse for Ollie to prepare for the rest of the crew, and the remainder would stay in the largest freezer chest in the larder off the back of the kitchen until distribution. Thus the mystery of the Thanksgiving turkey was solved, and another puzzle piece fell into place. Between the two of them, they were able to make short work of cramming the frozen holiday offerings into their temporary home to maintain their frigid state until delivery.

They still had some time before dinner to finish decorating the house. Jim accompanied Cutter to dinner, and she learned this was the case on the days Maria worked. It only made sense as Jim was often in Cutter's company, and Maria only had to prepare one meal. She was sure it also provided Cutter with company. Other than Jim and Sam, he kept an employer's distance from most of the rest of the crew.

*****

The following day, Lexie accompanied her husband on his turkey delivery route where she met a few more women she hadn't known existed on the ranch. The last stop was to a church in a small town to the north of the ranch. There he dropped off ten of the turkeys, as well as a hefty donation. Hard times in the town had swelled the need for the meals provided by the church volunteers.

During that outing, Lexie found herself reflecting on the events in Cutter's life that Maria had shared with her over the last couple of days, and how they contributed to the personality quirks of her husband.

Sam had told her that Maria was hysterical about having killed another dog, so Lexie asked her about it. The story that the cook related sent a chill up Lexie's spine.

"Cutter's mom died in childbirth with a little girl less than eighteen months from the time of his brother Ben's birth. Ben was breech and a C-section delivery. My mother told me years later 'Lynette was on birth control, but evidently they weren't effective enough, 'cause she had a miscarriage only six months after delivering.' Mom held that her husband Rod killed her by not leaving her alone long enough to heal. Cutter was maybe five or six then. One of Lynette's last gifts to Cutter was a little beagle type puppy. I guess his father blamed himself for her death. My mother said that he withdrew from life and took to drink. I remember that he never had a kind word for his sons. Maybe he could see her in their inherited gray eyes and couldn't cope. I was a couple of years younger than Cutter and my mother was almost as hard and unforgiving as Rod Ross. All Cutter, Ben, and I had were each other. The year I turned five it became my assigned chore to gather the eggs from the chicken coop. I hated the chickens because they would peck at my hands and arms until they often bled. Momma would wring the necks of the ones that didn't lay anymore, and then she made me help her pluck them. I hated that, too."

Lexie glanced over to the driver's seat of the Yukon trying to imagine Cutter as a small child as she recalled more of Maria's strange tale.

"Close to one year later while I was collecting eggs the nasty rooster attacked me. I kicked him across the hen house and then wrung his neck, like I had seen my mother do. Some of the hens got worked up and started flapping and pecking at me and I sent three of them to join the rooster. Mom came out to see what all of the ruckus was. She dragged me into the house and used a switch on me, and then warned me that if I ever told anyone she would give me a real beating. Mom told

Cutter's father that Red Baron killed the chickens, and he shot the little dog."

"Cutter was devastated. He used to sit on the porch at night with the little dog on his lap and talk to it, like he used to talk to his mother. Cutter had been at school, but little Ben had been standing at the mudroom door when his father blew the dog's head off. He would wake up with terrible nightmares and climb in bed with Cutter for comfort. I didn't have anyone to comfort me from my nightmares and guilt. I never went in that henhouse again. My mother threatened me with the switch. I told her I hated her, but if she hit me again I would tell everyone she lied and killed Cutter's dog. That's the other dog I hurt without meaning to."

Lexie told Maria that she was only a child and not responsible for her mother's lies or Cutter's dad's knee-jerk response. However, the story had shed light on the bizarre absence of chicken on the menu at the Rocking R. She had to assume that the absence of turkeys in the story was the reason they were legitimate holiday fare. She had asked, "Maria, what happened to Cutter's little brother?"

"Little Ben died of a snake bite when he was only ten. Cutter wasn't the same after that. He rarely smiled and his once warm gray eyes took on a glacial appearance. There was no love lost between him and his father. Cutter had heard the gossip about his mother's death and he knew his dad had shot his dog. He also laid the blame squarely in his dad's lap for little Ben's death. Mr. Ross had sent his ten-year-old son to bring in firewood, and the child never saw the rattler. Ben was too terrified of his father and my mother to tell them that he had been bitten. He might have told Cutter, but his brother was mucking out stalls and Ben couldn't make it that far. He collapsed and died not even halfway to the old horse barn."

That explained quite a bit about her husband's possessiveness and his inability to express his feelings. Yet he was very articulate in his ranch and business dealings. Most business decisions didn't require an investment of emotion or heart and a loss was not likely to injure an already battered soul.

She was probably just as guilty in regards to guarding her heart, and if she hadn't reached out to Maria she still wouldn't have a clue to the extent of her husband's emotional baggage.

When they returned from the turkey delivery, Maria had steaks, Spanish rice, and a mixed vegetable medley ready. After dinner, they took the dogs out for a while to check on the progress of the run. It was up and fully functional. Pete had done a splendid job.

"I will probably have to find a dog house so they can have shelter from the hot sun or inclement weather, if they are in there any length of time."

******

The weather was a little cool on Saturday, but pleasantly so. The kitchen didn't heat up excessively while she and Maria worked on Christmas cookies. Sunday was another story. A light rain was the leading edge of a cold front and the precipitation turned to snow. Almost an inch of the white stuff blanketed the area one week before Christmas. Temperatures yo-yoed for the next few days, bringing alternating rain and a sleet-snow mix. The circling weather front and the resulting moisture were an early Christmas gift for the parched land and those who lived on it. Christmas day saw another bout of snowflakes, but by the day after, the whole system was on its way to the Tennessee and Ohio valleys.

Cutter had taken up where Lexie's mother and grandmother left off. He gave her a beautiful diamond and sapphire pendant with matching earrings. She hadn't a clue where she would ever wear them, but she loved them just the same. The thought occurred to her that they would complement her gray gown, if she could ever get into it again.

What can you get for a man who can buy failing farms at will? Lexie decided on useful and functional; she gave him a diver's watch, a new leather belt, a new cell phone carrier, and on a whim, a new blue plaid shirt to replace the one she'd adopted as sleepwear. Mom and Gram sent him a huge hand-made quilt in brown, green, and burgundy colors that matched the décor in their bedroom. That gift really seemed to move him. It was something that money couldn't buy; there was love in every stitch.

The normal routine picked up by Tuesday, and that morning Lexie asked what the Rocking R did for New Year's Eve. Maria's blank stare gave her the answer: nada. It was too late to organize anything for this year, but she had plenty of time to plan next year's party.

Before starting on the year-end reconciliations and tax prep, Lexie potted the dogs, then searched online for some deals on maternity clothes. Post-Christmas sales in stock were very limited, so she ordered what she liked on her credit card and had the items shipped. It was becoming impossible to zip up her jeans or fasten them; she was swelling up like a balloon. Her rings were even getting tight and uncomfortable; it took liquid soap along with a lot of pulling and twisting to remove them. She rinsed them off, dried them, and placed the rings in her small jewelry case on top of the dresser in their room before returning to the year-end tax issue.

Things went south quickly after lunch. First Cutter demanded to know where her rings were. Lexie didn't like his accusatory tone, so she told him she had pawned them. He didn't see any humor in her answer, so she broke down, and told him where they were and why. He went to look to be assured the rings were indeed where she had told him. She took her glass of tea and returned to the office willing her eyes not to tear up. "I'm so damned emotional lately" she told her canine pal.

Two hours later, Patrick Boyd phoned her. David Decker had been spotted in Oklahoma City. The sheriff had put out an extradition request, should the authorities in Oklahoma apprehend him. Patrick informed her, "We have a warrant out for him for kidnapping. The toxicology reports showed several doses of Rohypnol stashed in the bottom of an aspirin bottle taken from Decker's medicine cabinet. Xanax was also found in a non-prescription bottle retrieved from Mel's handbag."

The bottom line was that law enforcement had kept this information close to their vest once they found out the body retrieved from the rubble at the Lazy K was not David Decker. Once David was eliminated the forensic people went to work trying to identify the burn victim found in the in the shell of the ranch house. Mr. Potter had also hired a PI to track Decker. The investigator followed him from Miami back to Oklahoma, and Booker contacted Patrick with the information. Booker also notified her before the Deputy had that Decker was on the move and headed west.

The best the sheriff's office or other police could do was arrest him on the kidnapping charge. Mel would have to press charges and agree to testify; only then could the law attempt to lock him away. Patrick was of the opinion that prosecutors would be hard pressed to prove that Decker had drugged her.

The whole thing was depressing. Even if they arrested him, the courts would probably let him off. Lexie was certain of one thing. If the law didn't exact justice for Mel and her unborn child, Mr. Potter would.

CHAPTER 10

THE weather continued to be erratic for the next couple of days, and Lexie was going stir crazy. Her riding was curtailed to the indoor arena and Blue was suspiciously absent She had to make herself content with Blaze. Once their child was born, she was seriously going to find a horse of her own, and God help the person that put a hand on it.

She coerced Maria into joining her for a day in town, by citing the need to purchase some clothes that would fit her expanding waistline. The winter clothing she had brought along ended up being useless as a result of her new bulging form. "You know Cutter will have a royal tantrum if I go to Lubbock alone."

The two women roamed the stores for bargains to supplement what Lexie had purchased online that had not yet been delivered. Going up sizes was depressing. She and Maria went to lunch, and then to an afternoon movie in an effort to banish her persistent funk.

*****

David was having a covert meeting with a couple of local thieves that had joined forces with him a few times in the past. Both had connections with people who could fix him with up a multitude of narcotics. He had blown through the remainder of funds left from the sale of the ranch, after paying off his gambling debts. Moving drugs had the potential to be more profitable than a nine to five. A dark Suburban with Ohio plates caught his attention. He would know the blonde driver anywhere; she was the one responsible for messing up his plans, and sicking Melinda's dad on him. He was only passing through on his way south of the border when a new opportunity presented itself. He recognized the passenger as the longtime cook at the Rocking R. He speculated it must mean that Melinda's little pain-in-the-ass friend was in residence there. He'd heard she was working as a live-in bookkeeper, but had returned to Ohio before his intended fiancé and her father. He wondered what she doing in the area now?

David couldn't follow her. She would spot him in a nanosecond. Instead, he assigned Clint, the brighter of his two cohorts, to track her and find out what he could. Clint was an average-looking guy: a bit shy of six foot, slightly hefty with a receding nondescript brown hairline, and brown eyes that effectively let him blended in nicely. Hernando was much too seedy looking for this assignment. Taller than his partner, he was also a lot heavier, with black hair, dark eyes, and a perpetual black shadow of stubble on his face. He was great when it came to intimidation and dirty work, but he would draw too much attention for this job.

Remaining in one spot too long made David nervous. He was sure that the hapless look-alike that Clint and Hernando had followed out of a cantina near San Antonio had initially passed for him, but it paid to be careful. His two companions had shot up the ranch house to make it look like a hit on him covered up by the fire, but the word was Deputy Boyd was still looking into the suspicious fire. David was sure he was under surveillance while in Florida and figured the law had made a determination that he wasn't the body in his old burnt out shell of a home.

It was almost an hour later when Clint reappeared. As soon as he entered the back seat of the old dark blue Buick, Hernando eased in to traffic while Clint filled them in.

"I followed the two women around. They shopped for underwear, and then wandered over to check out the maternity department. The second store they entered had higher-end dresses. That was where they ran into to a man shopping with his pregnant wife. He greeted both of the women by name. The plump, dark-haired one he called Maria, but he was real polite when speaking with the little blonde who he called Mrs. Ross when he introduced his wife."

By the time the fugitive and his shady friends circled back to where Lexie had parked, the women were gone. If Cutter Ross finally took the plunge, he would pay plenty to get his wife and unborn child back. It was time to work out a plan of action, and then head for the border with their captive.

******

Lexie stashed her purchased expectant mommy clothes, then potted the dogs and fed them before pitching in to make the salad for dinner. She set the table while Maria worked on the steaks and baked yams. They had stopped at the bakery where Maria purchased more of the heavenly hard rolls, and Lexie bought a yummy-looking carrot cake for their desert. There goes another dress size, briefly flitted through her mind when she had purchased the confection.

Dinner was a big hit, and neither Cutter nor Jim had a clue that they'd thrown the meal together in approximately thirty minutes.

Friday morning, Lexie entered the few remaining invoices for the year, and then made out the payroll checks. The checks were now ready for Cutter to sign after lunch and distribute later that afternoon. Dinner was a little more involved than the day before, and they were back to the Tex-Mex fare. Their husbands went back out to attend to some ranch chore or another following several helpings of dessert. It was getting dark when they returned to find Lexie kneading bread dough at the kitchen table while Maria placed the finished product in loaf pans. That was one of the last normal chores of their day.

Cutter and Jim were about to call it quits for the day when shouts from the cookhouse sent them on a run out the door. Bright flames lit up the night sky to the east. Cutter had stopped back at the house long enough to warn her "Lexie, if Sam tells you to evacuate, you and Maria get out!"

He sure was good at barking orders, but he was even better at kissing her breathless before he ran from the house. In a flash, most of the men were following in Cutter's wake as the ranch pickup roared out of her view toward the fire. She prayed that nothing happened to him or anyone else. Fire was a tricky thing, especially if the wind kicked up.

Sam and Pete were left to evacuate the horses, should the fire spread in their direction.

Maria had set the last of the bread loaves to rise, and was cleaning up what remained of the dinner pots and pans in addition to their floury bread-making mess.

"Maria, I am going to change my flour caked shirt before I pot the dogs."

Lexie had barely put on a clean shirt when she heard Maria scream; the first thing that came to her mind was the horse and/or the hay barns were on fire. She ran up the hall returning to the kitchen, and then skidded to an abrupt halt. There, she came face to face with a man holding a gun on Maria. It took her a few seconds to recognize the home invader as David Decker; his face was bearded and he wore dark tinted glasses under a battered tan Stetson.

David hadn't expected Maria to still be at the ranch this time of the evening. The fire diversion had worked fine, and he'd waited for the men to be several miles away before entering the house. It would have been much simpler if his quarry had been alone; now, he had the cook to deal with. He kept the gun on Maria. Her panicked scream had brought his intended prey running straight to him. He ordered the new Mrs. Ross, "You come over here; we are going for a ride."

"Not damn likely, Decker."

Lexie heard a low, threatening growl, and fired off a few commands, "Sie ruhig! Bleib wachsam, wir haben einen Eindringling!" praying that the intruder didn't understand German.

"What did you just say?"

"I was just cussing you out in my grandmother's native tongue."

"Well, try this on for size. If you don't come over here I am going to shoot your cook."

"Go ahead and shoot her. I am sick to death of her jalapeño-laced meals."

He wasn't expecting her to give up the other woman. David noticed that her hands were missing the wedding rings he had heard could pay off a good part of the national debt.

"Where are your rings?"

"Why?"

"If we don't have your rings, the only other way we can convince your husband we have you and that he should pay the ransom would be to remove one of your fingers to send him."

She glared at him while jutting her defiant chin, but the cook fainted dead away. He moved around the Hispanic lump on the floor and closed the space between himself and Cutter's belligerent wife.

Lexie didn't believe Maria, who dressed wounds, and had wrung chicken's necks as a child, would faint at the thought of someone else losing a finger. She backed away from his advance to draw him away from Maria's prone form.

David felt more confident with her retreat. Maybe she was more scared than she let on? He pointed the gun at her for added intimidation. He had no intention of shooting her, though it was tempting. She wasn't of any use to him dead. "Last chance, bitch. Where are your rings?"

"They're in the wall safe in the ranch office across the hall, with the other valuables and what cash we have on hand." She was improvising, trying to delay the inevitable. Decker should have never entered this house, and he was going to pay for it dearly if she could manipulate him to the other side of the house.

He didn't trust her. "Why are your rings in the safe and not on your finger?"

"We were baking bread and I didn't want to get dough in the settings."

He glanced in the direction she waved her hand, and sure enough, pans of dough were lined up waiting to be baked. It only took that moment of distraction to send him ducking the cast iron skillet aimed at his head. Instead, the potentially deadly skillet impacted his shoulder, and the gun went off.

As soon as Lexie latched on to the heavy skillet, aiming it at his head, she ordered Maria to run for it. Damn! I missed his head, she thought. The sound of the shot reverberated off the walls and inside her head, but she felt a stabbing pain in her left shoulder.

David was really fighting the urge to finish off the witch— his shoulder was killing him where the iron pan had smashed into it—but he needed her to access the safe. It would be easier to clean out the safe than deal with this crazy woman. "Bist du bereit zu ihn angreifen! Vorschict, pass auf! Er hat eine Waffe!" Cutter's harpy was cussing him out in German again. He reached across to grab her, and then slapped her across the face. David took a fistful of her blonde tresses and forced her across the hall. Little did he know that he was playing right into her hands. It was obvious to her he hadn't understood a word she'd said, and she had succeeded with making her commands sound like cuss words.

David was losing patience and running out of time. "Open the door and be quick about it."

Lexie was trying to stall, hoping Maria could avoid his companion and reach Sam. She also prayed there was only one other culprit standing guard. David had said "we", meaning he was not alone in this kidnap attempt. She turned with her back to the door and warned him "You don't want to go through with this David. Cut your losses and leave now."

That little speech cost her a blow with the butt of his gun on the left side of her forehead, only two inches above her temple. She fumbled with the doorknob, frustrating him to the point that he opened it himself and shoved her in before him. Lexie used the momentum of his push to fall to the floor. David's gun fell to the floor beside her as he fought off over a hundred pounds of canine fury. David was propelled backward into the hall by Skip's collision with his chest. Her dog had him down and was intent on reaching his jugular.

At that point, she must have blacked out. Lexie heard Sam's voice, but she didn't recall him arriving.

"Lexie, call the dogs off!"

She called for Skip; he returned to sit beside her, but she didn't know that the puppies had joined in the attack, following the lead of their mentor. Fortunately, they were small enough that Maria was able to pluck them off David's writhing form.

Sam and Pete took the injured house invader and would-be kidnapper to the cookhouse to bind his wounds and wait for the sheriff.

Cutter and Jim were there before the sheriff or the medical helicopter dispatched by Doctor Callahan. Maria had been busy after her hasty departure from the kitchen battlefield. After summoning Sam and Pete, she notified Cutter, and then the doctor.

******

Lexie woke once more in a hospital bed in Amarillo. At first she thought the past six and a half months had all been in her mind, but this room was different. She was in recovery, and again hooked up to an IV.

She looked around for a familiar face, but when she found none she closed her eyes and drifted back to sleep. Her next sojourn to reality lasted most of the early morning hours and well past breakfast. Her private room must have been a clone of the one from which she had escaped in June. She wondered whether it was the same room or only appeared to be.

Dr. Callahan arrived shortly after the removal of the breakfast tray.

"How are we doing this morning, Lexie?"

She always found it extremely irritating when medical people used "we", like they were really in the same situation. "I don't know about you, Doc, but I feel pretty lousy—like someone shot me and tried to cave in my skull."

"I wasn't referring to you and me, but you and your unborn child. I can order some ibuprofen to ease your pain, but I hesitate to give you anything too strong. It could cause issues with fetus. We only gave you a local to remove the bullet and stitch up your head wound."

"What's with the IV?"

"One is saline, the other is plasma. You lost a lot of blood and the paramedics needed to stabilize you during transport; we opted to keep the feed going during surgery and recovery. If you check out okay, we will most likely disconnect both later today."

After he checked her vitals and her wounds, he sat down in the chair and lowered the boom. "You need to take better care of yourself; confronting gun-wielding thugs is not an activity for a pregnant lady."

"I suppose you think I should have gone meekly along with his kidnap plans. Sorry, Doc, but if I am going out, I'm going out fighting."

"I kind of figured that, but why is it I am only now finding out you are expecting?"

"No offense, Doc, but I preferred a woman physician and one that didn't know Cutter."

"Well, I need to have her name so we can coordinate your care."

Lexie reluctantly gave him the doctor's name as well as the clinic address. She closed her eyes and blocked out the constant hospital hustle and bustle. Doctor Callahan told her the fatigue was due to blood loss and her body trying to recoup from the trauma as well as surgery. This was not the way she'd figured on spending New Year's Eve. She sure hoped 2012 progressed more smoothly than 2011 had.

******

Patrick Boyd arrived to a scene of chaos and gore. He quickly stepped around the blood-spattered area of the hall to check on the status of Lexie Parker-Ross. She was cradled in Cutter's arms while he pressed a folded, once-white, towel to her shoulder wound. Jim had met Patrick and his partner as soon as they parked in the drive. Sam and Pete had Decker confined to the cookhouse. Boyd was unable to trust himself not to shoot Decker on the spot. Rather than personally taking custody of Decker, he sent Deputy Smith to secure the prisoner while he tried to help in the house. Before he could offer assistance, he needed to secure the crime scene. The dogs must have taken exception to his tone of voice when he ordered the occupants of the house to stay clear of the blood-splattered area, so as not to contaminate any evidence. The big, blood-soaked Shepherd growled threateningly, but didn't leave Mrs. Ross's side.

However, his warning didn't go unheeded by two small black pups—one with a cast on its front leg—that immediately attacked Patrick's pant leg. Fortunately, the tall western boots protected his leg. "Will someone confine these ankle biters somewhere?"

Maria once again scooped up the puppies, but this time she closed them in the bedroom that used to be where Lexie slept. She was not brave enough to try to remove Skip, and neither was anyone else.

When the paramedics moved Cutter out of the way so they could attend to his wife, he latched on to Skip's collar and hauled the reluctant dog away from Lexie. Patrick seized the opportunity to have Cutter cut a few of the blood-soaked hairs from the dog's chest, and place them in an evidence bag.

Cutter accompanied his wife on the life-flight chopper, and the big dog continued to sit out where the metal bird had carried of his mistress, looking off in the direction the noisy metal bird had flown.

Patrick was grateful that Cutter was no longer there when Deputy Smith loped in like a modern day Barney Fife to report two more injuries, and the suspect nowhere to be found. Patrick put out an APB on Decker; the chances were he was going to need medical attention judging from the blood loss and description of his wounds provided by two ranch hands with major headaches.

Pete had been trying to wrap up David's wounds when he was hit from behind, and Sam had been knocked unconscious by the larger of the of Decker's accomplices; still, he was able to give a rudimentary description of the two assailants. Jim drove Sam and Pete to Lubbock for medical treatment while the deputies documented the mess on the previously pristine floor, and debriefed Maria. She walked Deputy Boyd through the events from the time Decker burst through the mudroom door, taking her hostage until she ran for help.

*****

Cutter had known as soon as they arrived at the site of the old Lazy K ranch house that the blaze had been deliberately set, but it didn't minimize the hazard. If the wind had kicked up again like it had the past few days, the embers would spread the fire for miles. The recent rains and melting snowfall were a godsend, but they were a long way from being out of the woods. Rubble not yet removed had been piled high, resembling a celebratory bonfire; fumes from the gas accelerant still lingered in the night air.

A panicked call from Maria that Lexie had been shot sent him and Jim racing back to the ranch. The pair of somber husbands left the others behind to finish the extinguishing of the fire. The scene that greeted them on their arrival would remain imprinted in Cutter's mind until his dying day. His small, feisty wife was lying in a wounded heap on the office floor. Maria was trying to clean up Lexie's bloody face while an equally bloody Skip stood guard. Cutter moved in to take over the task of caring for his wife. The head wound wasn't too bad, but bleeding profusely. A lump was rising, and it was going to take a few stitches. Of more concern was the blood flowing from the gunshot wound.

He had to caution the paramedics about what they gave her. Poor Skip didn't want to leave her any more than he did. Her dog was still in the same spot when Cutter finally returned home the afternoon of the following day. Once Lexie was out of recovery and safely out of harm's way, he'd called Jim for a ride home. His foreman and friend provided an update on events after he and Lexie had flown off in the helicopter.

"Evidently, Sophie's no-good grandson had a couple of side-kicks for his planned abduction. They waylaid Sam and Pete making a clean get-away with David Decker. Patrick Boyd was livid that Decker had slipped through his fingers again. The Sheriff's office, the Texas Rangers, border patrol, and law enforcement in neighboring states all have descriptions not only of the suspects, but also a detailed account of the dog bite injuries to Decker. If he tries to get medical assistance, they have a good chance to nab him."

"You know, Jim, there are doctors who deal with gunshots, knife wounds, and the like off the books and out of the mainstream. He might already be patched up enough to have made it to Mexico. How are Sam and Pete doing?"

"Sam has a dislocated jaw, but he is down at the Sheriff's office going over mug shots. The clinic sent Pete over to the hospital for a couple of days of observation to monitor his concussion."

Cutter cleaned up the Shepherd and himself. He had some lunch, but couldn't convince the dog to eat or drink. After a brief nap, he snatched the precious quilt Lexie's grandmother had made for her, and Skip's seldom-used leash before heading back to see his wife. Getting Skip into the Yukon was a chore; once he was back outdoors he took up his vigil, scanning the sky for the helicopter that had whisked away the focus of his life.

******

Lexie finished her dinner and turned on the TV. She was hoping to catch something on the news about Decker's arrest, but all the channel surfing produced zero. She opted for the country music channel to occupy her. She hadn't seen Cutter all day, but she'd been assured by Doc Callahan that her husband had been with her all night, and only left after she was declared out of danger and on the road to recovery.

She didn't even have her phone to call home to wish her mother and grandmother a Happy New Year. The landline had been removed from her room, and she wondered if it was cost reduction move on the part of number crunchers, or if the doctor and her husband had ordered it taken out. Lexie decided to give them the benefit of the doubt. She'd heard on the news hospital administrators in some areas were making reductions to the old phone in every room. The rationalization was that everyone now used cell phones. That was all fine and dandy if you happened to have one. Otherwise, patients needed to use a phone at one of the designated nursing stations or information desks. At least one positive thing happened between lunch and dinner. Her IV was removed, which made trips to the small bathroom on the other end of the room much less of an ordeal.

She'd barely made it back under the covers after such a journey when her husband appeared in the doorway. He peeked around the partially closed door to scan the room.

"Can we come in?"

Lexie wondered who the "we" referred to. She was delighted to see Skip. Cutter unhooked him and closed the door. Skip made a beeline for her. She sat on the edge of the bed ruffled his hair and hugged him. "That's my brave boy!" She praised him while taking a closer look at the vest he was wearing. It had a round patch with a blue cross that was decorated down the middle with a medical caduceus. The red letters that encircled the emblem centered on the white background boldly stated, "Service Dog Access Required". She noticed her husband remove his sunglasses as he entered the room from the darkness of a starlit night.

"How did you get the service dog vest?" she asked, trying to choke back the laughter bubbling up at the vision of Cutter playing a sight impaired person in need of a service dog to bring Skip up for a visit with her. She was touched by the gesture.

I bought it off of a real service dog's handler this morning on the way out. Fortunately, that dog was very large, too."

Lexie lost it and laughed so hard at his rendition of the ruse to bring Skip to see her that her shoulder began to throb. Her mirth was quickly contained when Cutter explained that Skip had still been in the same spot as the previous night waiting for her return. Her husband unwrapped a small bowl and a plastic bag filled with kibble from the folds of her quilt. He shook the quilt out before placing it on the bed.

"I thought you might like to have it while you're here." He kissed her soundly, and then went to fill Skip's bowl with water. "He refused to eat or drink. I literally had to drag him away to wash off the dried blood, and then force him into the vehicle to bring him here. Thankfully, he put up with the annoyance, and didn't take a chunk out of me. Jim and Maria took the other puppies home with them last night, but Skip growled and bared his teeth when they tried to remove him from his post, so they reluctantly left him there for the night."

The canine under discussion wandered over to lap water from the bowl and try some of the dried food that Cutter had sprinkled on the floor.

"I guess he's content and hungry now that he knows you're all right."

Cutter had brought a deck of cards in his stash of New Year's Eve goodies. They played rummy, talked, and half listened to the TV countdown party. Lexie was disappointed that Decker had once again escaped the clutches of the law and was probably well south of the border by now. But Cutter, Sam, Pete, and Maria had all made statements and filed charges. If and when David Decker set foot in the States again he would most likely be apprehended or shot. Lexie would feel a lot better when he was in jail, and she would definitely testify against him. Unlike Mel, she had plenty of other witnesses to his assault and attempted kidnapping.

Husband and wife kissed in 2012 and tilted the world on its axis—at least it felt that way to Lexie. Before he and Skip went home for the remainder of the night, Cutter pulled her little phone from his jacket pocket and handed it to her. She let out a barely audible giggle when he said he had to go before their celebration got out of hand. Thanks to her considerate husband, she was able to wish in the New Year with her grandmother and Mel. It seemed that her mother was out at a New Year's Eve bash with Booker. She settled for leaving a voicemail greeting for her mom.

Lexie had plenty of company on New Year's Day: Cutter and his service dog returned, Jim and Maria came by, Sam and Pete dropped in to see her, and Patrick Boyd even made an appearance.

She was released on the third, after a consultation with her new O.B. G.Y.N. and Dr. Callahan.

She was given a prescription for a diuretic to combat the water retention, and to help with the swelling of her hands and feet. "Great! I'm going to blow up like Harry Potter's nasty aunt!"

Her new female doctor, Irene Gomez, who had been referred through the clinic that Lexie'd been attending, told her to drink plenty of liquids including water. It seemed the more she drank the less likely her body would be to retain fluid. She was also told to walk as much as possible. Lexie figured that would be covered in more frequent trips to relieve herself, if she was to increase her fluid intake.

******

Early February the rains came, and snow too! Temperatures hovered in the thirties. Lexie felt the baby move, and decided it was time to let her mom and grandma know. She waited until closer to Valentine's Day, and then sent them each a card elevating the usual greeting to Grandma Eve and Great-grandma Jane. She wasn't sure what to do about Melinda. Her friend had been devastated at the loss of her unborn child, and Lexie was afraid the news would bring back unhappy memories. She settled for signing Mel's card as always, but adding an invitation to visit her and her new family that summer.

The phone calls began the day before the official holiday. First, Mom called, and Lexie was on the phone for a good hour trying to explain why she hadn't let them know earlier. Then, she had to explain it all again to Grandma. A lot of it was fabrication, but she didn't want them to know about the incident with Decker for fear it would get back to Mel. On the hearts and candy day, Mel called; she had heard the news from Lexie's broadcasting mother. She sure hoped Booker didn't share anything with her mom that he didn't want spread to half the town.

A case of anti-stretch mark cream arrived a week later from her mother. Her note of instructions read; "To be applied daily by the culprit responsible." Cutter enthusiastically adhered to the instructions, making for some interesting foreplay they both enjoyed. He would linger over swollen abdomen longer as their child became more active and he could feel the movement. Occasionally, he would get a swift kick in the palm of his large calloused hand. His expression was priceless and would usually cause her to break out in delighted laughter.

Things were progressing well at the Rocking R. The rain barrels were better than half full. Maria and Lexie had come to an accord, and little Alex, now twice her previous size, was running like she'd never had a broken leg. Maria fell in love with the brave little pup the night that she, cast and all, had joined in the attack on Decker and then decided she was going after Patrick Boyd. Alex seemed to return Maria's affection, which prompted Lexie agreed to the cook's request to adopt the pup. All four abandoned puppies found good homes. Cutter would often sit in one of the armchairs in the evening with Bib in his lap while he attempted to teach his wife the game of chess.

Late March saw another unexpected delivery to the Rocking R's kitchen in the form of hams. Lexie accompanied her husband on his pre-Easter rounds, much as she had done back in December on the turkey run. She finally got him to admit to her that he paid out of his own funds for the annual gifts, and that was the reason she didn't have any invoices for the purchases. She also gained the knowledge that Cutter had always paid cash for the turkeys and hams for the better part of a decade. The practice of delivering a holiday turkey for the crew once a year had begun when his father ran the place and at that time they went through the accounts as a Christmas bonus. After his father literally drank himself to death, Cutter changed the practice. That was another discrepancy in Bob Henson's books. He'd continued to enter the turkeys and hams as paid out of cash funds from the ranch operating accounts. Lexie figured the old bookkeeper had found a way to pocket a substantial sum twice a year. She intended to have an accredited CPA verify her findings before she again brought the subject up with her husband.

Lexie didn't get out much after Easter. She stopped riding and had to force herself to walk the dogs a couple of times a day to get a modicum of exercise. She was getting huge! It became more difficult to carry her burden the farther along the pregnancy progressed. She was sure she had to be carting around twins, but Dr. Irene performed another ultrasound and assured her there was only one very large baby boy. The next nine and a half weeks allowed her to near completion of her CPA classes. Once the baby was born, a quick review should be sufficient for her to sit for the exam. She still held that she may need the skill somewhere down the line and remained reluctant to be entirely dependent on her husband.

After ten hours of blinding pain and some-no-so-complimentary expletives aimed at her husband, little Benjamin Cutter Ross made his debut. He weighed in at a whopping nine pounds and two ounces. No wonder he had felt like he was going to fall out the front of her the last few weeks! It was Cutter who brought up the coincidence of their child's birthday.

"Lex, do you realize it was one year ago today that I pulled you out of the mud and brought you home with me?"

"Truthfully, I don't remember much after you and Jim pulled the calf out of the muck, but I guess it was fate or something."

Lexie loved her big-hearted husband who did his best to hide that heart beneath a gruff, no-nonsense, exterior. She was more positive than ever a woman could never know when or where the love of her life might show up.

EPILOGUE

Two-year-old Ben Ross visited with his godparents while his mom and dad made the trip to Lubbock International to pick up their houseguests. Lexie's mother and grandmother were due to arrive shortly, but you never could tell about airline departures or arrivals any longer. It would have been too much for their active little son—the long drive and the inevitable wait at the airport.

Eve's nerves were raw, and her mother's constant complaining about the decline of the airline industry was not helping her condition. She was having second thoughts about Booker. He made her feel young again. It had been a long time since she had a serious relationship with a man. She'd met Booker while planning her daughter's wedding to Cutter Ross. Now, it was her turn to walk down the aisle. She hoped things would not be as tumultuous for her and Booker as her daughter's relationship was with her tall Texan.

Lexie was the reason for the plane trip to the Texas panhandle. Eve had made the mistake of informing her daughter that Booker had proposed. Eve's daughter had grabbled the bull by the horns, so to speak, and made arrangements to have the wedding at a small church near the ranch that she and her little family attended. Mom and she would be staying at her daughter and son-in-law's home until the pending nuptials. Mom would be remaining to visit while Eve and Booker went on a two-week honeymoon. She sure hoped that Lexie knew what she was doing. Mom wasn't as spry as she used to be, but she was as opinionated and quarrelsome as ever.

Booker had driven them to Hopkins, and then accompanied them to baggage check-in. That was where they parted company; it was as far as anyone not on the flight could go. The security measures set Mom off on the good old days when family or friends could wait in the boarding area and see the plane leave the gate. She'd been on a rant since, and Eve thought that maybe her mother could be nervous about flying. Booker would be arriving in Lubbock tomorrow with the Potters in their private jet. That was Lexie's doing, too. She'd immediately switched from matron of honor to bridesmaid when she found out that Booker had asked Patrick Boyd to be his best man. Lexie relinquished the honored spot, using the excuse that she could pair up with her husband who was Booker's only choice as an usher. Eve couldn't shake the feeling that her daughter and her soon-to-be groom were teamed up as an unlikely pair of matchmakers. Eve had been back for little Benjamin's christening, and again last June for his birthday, but Melinda hadn't returned since the summer the girls graduated from Ohio State.

******

Cutter questioned his wife as he pulled their new silver Yukon in to a parking spot near the terminal. "Are you sure you know what you're doing, Lex?"

"Grandma will only be with us for a couple of weeks, and I gave Maria a heads-up about her personality quirks. You'll be out of the house most of the day. She shouldn't make you too crazy."

"I wasn't referring to your grandmother and you damned well know it! I was talking about involving Melinda in the wedding party. You know how reluctant she's been to return to Texas."

"Don't growl at me, Cutter. I didn't want to return either, but that didn't stop you from eliciting help from my family and friends to change my mind. And don't bother telling me that was different, because it's not."

Cutter rolled his eyes toward the heavens as his wife exited the vehicle and headed for the terminal. She may have her mother's sense of style and salty language, but she was much more of a personality match to her cantankerous grandmother. The mere thought of living his old age with a carbon copy of Lexie's grandmother brought about an involuntary shudder. He caught up with his wife moments before she entered the terminal. Cutter had a feeling she was up to something, but he knew from bitter experience that if Lexie had a secret she would keep it.

****

The story of Cutter, Lexie, their, family, and friends continue in **"Firestorms of the Heart" Book 3 of the "Troubles in Love-Land" Series** coming soon. Will Eve Parker make the wedding date with Booker or will her doubts overtake her?

Decker's hatred of Lexie knows no bounds. Will he leave the relative safety of Mexico to seek vengeance, and who was the dead man found in the burned out ranch house?

If you enjoyed "Panhandle Mayhem" please take a moment to review it.

Drop a note or sign up for my quarterly newsletter at tales-byjackie@gmail.com.

Thank you for choosing this book.

Excerpt: Firestorms of the Heart

One more beer then I'll find a bed for the night, he thought. A vehicle backfired and Jon dove for cover beneath the shabby, cracked, brown vinyl padded barstool. Sweat poured down his back, while violent tremors wracked his body. Transported to a desert half a world away, he struggled to right himself. All was silent, but the blast kept echoing between his fractured eardrums. Women with long dresses and head coverings snatched up screaming injured babies and toddlers, crying children stumbled among the ruins and the broken bodies.

Blood mingled with the sweat soaking him; the whole scene was horrifying and other worldly, but silent like the old time silent movies. Sergeant Jonathon Morgan scrambled over the remains of the village, keeping low while checking the injuries of the rest of his ambushed patrol. Voices penetrated once more! He decided that maybe he wasn't totally deaf….

"Hey, Jon, buddy are you okay?"

He gazed around the barstool toward the somewhat familiar voice. He thought was safe, home once more in San Antonio.

"Hey, buddy, let us buy you a drink. It sure looks like you could use one." Clint offered the big guy a hand to help him rise from the floor.

"Thanks." Jon slurred his gratitude for the assist while remounting the stool. "I reckon one more drink for the road couldn't hurt." He tried to remember their names.

A week earlier, Jon had run into Clint, in this very bar—just a case of mistaken identity. Clint had slapped him on the back and called him David and Jon decked the shorter man sending his eyeglasses skidding across the floor when Clint put his hands on Jon's still healing shrapnel wounds; his combat training took over. That was the first beer that Clint had bought him. Evidently, Jon looked enough like their friend David to be mistaken for him.

That Wednesday night and two beers later Clint offered to drive Jon to the hotel. "Man, you don't look like you can make the trip hoofing it."

Jon accepted the ride. The beer had hit him hard that evening, and he couldn't remember whether or not he had taken his meds. He followed Clint out the front door and around the side of the building to the parking lot.

ABOUT THE AUTHOR

Ms. Anton is busy at work on the third and forth books of the "Troubles in Love-Land Series. Look for "Firestorms of the Heart." To be released by Jan. of 2016. "A Second Chance" will be released in March of 2016.

Don't overlook J. M. Anton's adult novel "Wind River Refuge. This Mystery/Thriller with a paranormal twist and an unusual love story won the "Indie Next Generation Book Award" in the Romance Category.

Keep your eyes on your favorite E-book outlet for "Cassandra: Night Shades. Due October 31, 2015.

www.ingramcontent.com/pod-product-compliance
Lightning Source LLC
Chambersburg PA
CBHW021021120726
47905CB00009B/3122